A SPELL OF MURDERS

Karl M. King

Grosvenor House
Publishing Limited

The right of Karl M. King to be identified as the author of this
work has been asserted in accordance with Section 78
of the Copyright, Designs and Patents Act 1988

The book cover picture is copyright to Karl M. King
Cover Design by cheriefox.com

This book is published by
Grosvenor House Publishing Ltd
Link House
140 The Broadway, Tolworth, Surrey, KT6 7HT.
www.grosvenorhousepublishing.co.uk

This book is a work of fiction. Any resemblance to
people or events, past or present, is purely coincidental.

A CIP record for this book
is available from the British Library

ISBN 978-1-80381-000-3

Dedication
For Mum, Dad, Moira, Lucy & Matthew
Couldn't have done this without you

Prologue

"When you're in love with a beautiful woman, you watch her eyes."

He sang along cheerfully to the tune on the radio as he pulled the car into the nearest parking space. Not that it mattered much; the great thing about Redcar seafront at this time of night was that there was never any trouble parking.

He slid out of the car like a huge inelegant slug and pulled the large, grey, knee-length coat around himself to keep out the crisp night air. Walking round to the back of the car, he popped the boot open, lifted out the large duffel bag and threw it over his shoulder. He grunted at the heavy weight now weighing him down but ploughed on to his destination.

It was dark so he raised his staff, reached into it with his will, and bellowed, "Illumito!" This caused the end to set itself alight. The flame glowed brightly in the pitch black of the starless night like a small inferno. He didn't worry about being seen; the seafront was well away from the main drag and the crisp sea air made sure that it was too cold for any would-be lovers to risk an attempt at skinny dipping. He continued to whistle the tune cheerfully as he walked toward the old uneven stone steps that led down to the beach. "When you're in love with a beautiful woman, da de da da."

He took his time walking down the path to enjoy the salty sea air and the almost silent scuff of his shoes on the sand-covered pavement. When he reached the steps, he started to descend them slowly and deliberately. He soon reached the bottom and was walking toward the middle of the beach. The tide was out but the sand was still wet and squelched underneath his feet. Damn, he'd have to clean his shoes when he got home. He tossed the bag down in the middle of the open expanse of sand and started to retrace his steps.

Once he reached the top of the pier, he looked down onto the sand, at the footprints that led to the strange black mass that now lay in the middle of the beach. Reaching into his coat, he removed a small pouch. Clumsily he tucked the staff under his left arm and grabbed a handful of white powder from within the pouch with his right hand. He raised it to his mouth and slowly uncurled his fingers, muttering the words, "Nifalto, unfino." The powder dispersed out from his palm like a living mist and spread down the steps and along the beach, following the exact path that he had just trodden. As it passed, a small but strong force like a miniature tornado followed in its wake, sweeping the sand up and then relaying it. When it reached the bag, it stopped and the sand settled completely flat as if nobody had ever been there.

He gave a wry smile as he returned the pouch to his coat pocket, then carried on whistling as he headed back to his car while twirling the staff in his hand.

The media reported the next day that the sixth victim had been discovered on Redcar beach by an early morning jogger. She'd been found in a dark blue duffel bag and was in the same condition as all the previous ones.

Chapter 1

"And as you can see, it's just like the other victims. Repeated stab wounds as if the killer was in a frenzy. Like the other female victims, she was also sexually assaulted and her heart, as well as most of her other organs, have been badly mutilated…"

Amy dashed away from the autopsy table and managed to reach the sink just in time. When she finished, she found herself wondering why the hell there would be a sink in a pathology lab, then she realised why and threw up again.

"Here you go, luv." Amy looked up. The coroner, a short balding man with grey hair, was holding a paper towel. She snatched it from him to show that she didn't approve of the sexism and threw in a dirty look for good measure.

"Thanks," she said sullenly as she wiped her mouth. "Where is everyone?"

The old man smirked. "They've gone upstairs."

Amy threw the soiled towel in a nearby peddle bin and made her way to the door, trying hard not to look at the autopsy table as she dashed past. She was going to kill Dave; he'd done that on purpose!

She found herself alone in the lift and started to pace around, running her hand through her long brown hair and fiddle with her curls like she always did when she was agitated. God, this was worse than she thought; she knew the freak was nuts but this was terrible. That made six victims now, two men and four women; how could he butcher them so badly? Hell, she should know that, it was the reason she was here, for Heaven's sake!

She checked herself over in the reflective surface of the lift walls and was relieved to see that her little 'discharge' hadn't spoilt the small amount of make-up she wore or caused her to crease her perfectly pressed business suit. She always felt that it was vital to keep a professional appearance at all times when working, especially during this, her first solo assignment. She never carried a handbag, preferring to keep her wallet in her pockets – if it was good enough for men, it was good enough for her. Unfortunately, it also meant she had no spare make-up to carry out repairs if they'd been needed.

The lift doors finally opened and she stepped out onto the fifth floor. It looked like any other open-plan office in any other business, all blue nylon carpet, shared desks and computers. Except that this was no accountancy firm; it was a special police task force that had been set up to catch a dangerous killer.

Amy looked around and finally noticed her brother standing in the corner of the office talking to another police officer. The other man wasn't someone she recognised, but then again, she still hadn't really met anyone in CID except Dave and his sergeant. Whoever this new guy was, he was taller than her brother. He must have been over six feet tall and Dave was no shorty at five eleven. The stranger was a tall black guy with a completely bald head and a smooth face that had soft features and a warm kind look. This was quite a contrast to Dave with his wavy brown hair and rough features, and even rougher manner, in Amy's opinion!

The only thing that the two men had in common were the equally smart dark blue business suits that they were both wearing.

Not giving any thought as to who the stranger was, Amy strode over to them and yelled for attention, "Dave! We need to talk."

Her brother looked up. "Not now, sis. Chief Inspector Williams and I have things to discuss."

"Oh really and who's he?"

Chief Inspector Williams smiled warmly and extended his hand. "Sorry, ma'am, I don't believe we've been formally introduced. I've just been temporarily transferred from London. Detective Chief Inspector Frank Williams."

He was as well spoken as he was well dressed, with a very kind demeanour and great warmth in his voice. Amy couldn't help but feel herself blush slightly as she shook his hand. He was so tall that she felt even shorter than usual; she almost felt that her neck was right back at a right angle as she looked up at him!

"Nice to meet you, Inspector. I'm Dr Amy Walsh."

"Oh, pleased to meet you. What brings you here?"

"Ahem." Dave made sure that the clearing of his throat was audibly heard by all. "If you don't mind, Frank, Amy is my little sister. She's just here visiting me."

"Just visiting you!" Amy was still annoyed and had had enough of being subtle.

"Look, sis, if you'll come with me, I've got your stuff in here."

"What stu—" Dave put his arm round her shoulder and expertly spun her around and pulled her into the nearest door. It turned out to be an empty interview room and her brother slammed the door behind them. "What is your problem?" she asked, starting to get extremely irritated.

"You are, Amy. Do you know who that is?"

"Yeah, Detective Chief Inspector Frank Williams. He just said."

"And where did he say he was from?"

"London. Though I must admit he sounds more like he's from East London to me."

"Never mind that. What do you think he's doing here?"

"I assume he's helping out."

"Helping himself, more like."

Amy gave her brother a curious look. "What are you talking about?"

"He's allegedly been brought in because he's a trained criminologist who's got experience with serial killers."

"And what do you think he's here for if he's not here to help catch Mad Jack?"

Dave groaned. 'Mad Jack' was the press's cute little nickname for the bastard, a throwback to the infamous ripper, coupled with a recent pop culture icon. Dave gritted his teeth. "He's trying to take the investigation away from me."

Amy gave him a sceptical look. "You're paranoid."

"No, I'm realistic."

Amy sighed and shook her head. "Whatever. I don't care about what problems you have round here, just give me those case files."

"I'll get you them in a minute."

"No, now!"

"You're not my boss, Amy."

"No, I'm a private consultant who has been brought in by your department to produce a psychological profile on a serial killer and in order to do that I need to know everything about the case."

"I let you see the latest evidence firsthand, didn't I?"

Amy could have sworn he almost smirked as he said that. "Oh yeah. Hilarious."

"Well, haven't you got enough information on what a sick bastard he is now?"

"Don't act clever, Dave, it doesn't suit you! You know bloody well that it doesn't work like that."

Dave snorted in an attempt to stop his anger boiling over. "Look, sis, I know you've got a degree in psychology and even a bloody PhD in this profiling thing but try and see it from my point of view. I've been a copper for over 10 years and I know how things are done. I don't appreciate having an outsider come into my investigation and try to tell me how to catch criminals!"

"An outsider?"

"You know what I mean."

"Yeah, I know what you mean. You don't trust criminal profiling because you don't understand it. Well, like it or not, Dave, your superiors think differently. Now get me those damn files or I'm taking it up with your super." With that, Amy left the interview room with a slam of the door, leaving her brother to stand there to grind his teeth and clench his fists.

Chapter 2

Mike finished scribbling the last of the equation on the whiteboard and turned back to the half-full lecture theatre. "And that's the solution. Does anyone have any questions?" Silence. He smiled and glanced at his watch. "Right, okay then, I think that's enough for today. Remember we're having a mid-semester test next week and your lab reports are due on Friday. Dr Spence and I will be running a couple of tutorial sessions on this semester's work this Thursday. If anyone wants to attend, you're more than welcome. I'll be posting the details on the noticeboard tomorrow."

The students had already started to gather their books and bags. Realising he may as well have been talking to himself, Mike started to gather his own laptop and notes together. It always amazed him how few questions students had when it was the last lecture of the day, even when it was a complicated subject like quantum mechanics. True, the lecture he'd just given was on basic probability theory but that was beside the point!

He watched all the students make their way out the door at the back before he picked up his own materials. He'd always thought that it was important to wait until the entire class had left before he made his own exit, just in case anyone wanted to ask him anything in private. As usual, for the last lecture of the day, though, nobody stayed behind. He chuckled to himself as he followed the last of the students up the steps to the back of the theatre and out the door.

"Hey, Dr Walker." Mike jumped slightly and almost dropped his computer. The young woman had been waiting outside the door for him, but she seemed to think that the cleverest thing to do was to wait until he had come out and jump him from behind.

When he finally managed to rebalance everything he was carrying, Mike exhaled. "Tracy, don't do that. You could give someone a heart attack."

Tracy Chapman was currently Mike's only research student. She was tall, blonde and beautiful. Well, she was tall with dyed blonde hair and a face that was attractive. All traits that many would still think were unusual for a physics PhD student, but it just went to show that appearances could be deceptive. She smiled brightly at him and made a point to show all her teeth. "Sorry, Doc, feeling your age?"

"Hey I'm barely 10 years older than you and don't you forget it!"

"Ooh, touchy."

Mike exhaled again. The truth hurt. The fact was that he always had felt a bit self-conscious that his receding hair, round face and equally rounded out figure made him look older than his 31 years! His mum always told him that he was just insecure and that it was the only reason he always wore tee shirt and jeans instead of shirt and tie, even at work, but he refused to believe that.

That wasn't currently his only source of irritation, though. Tracy had a habit of getting under his skin, in more ways than one. She'd been his research student for two years now and was a good physicist, he supposed. She certainly had some interesting ideas about string theory but she had what Mike thought was a typical Southerner's attitude in that she thought she could get away with anything with good looks and enough front. Mike sometimes wondered if maybe he was just a bitter lad from the North, but Tracy certainly seemed to be more interested in going out and partying rather than writing her research papers. Mike often thought that she wanted to be one of those eternal students who'd hide from life by doing course after course and that annoyed him slightly. To him, academia was about more than the pieces of paper you got out of it. It was about respect, knowledge and a desire to understand more about what interested you. It wasn't just an excuse to hide from life. That really wound him up.

With Tracy, there was also of course the fact that she was an attractive young woman and to say that Mike didn't have the greatest track record of dealing with women, especially attractive ones, would probably be best classed as an understatement. Also, whether he liked to admit it or not, he did enjoy Tracy's company. Not only because she was good looking, but also because she was lively and exciting with an enthusiasm for life that could be infectious. She also had a sort of naivety about her that made her seem kind and sweet instead of manipulative. Mike often wondered which her true personality was. Hell, maybe it was neither or, more likely, maybe it was both!

Nevertheless, despite all that, Tracy was still his student and he was her supervisor so Mike wasn't going to put up with any funny business from her especially after she nearly frightened him half to death. He fixed her with a hard stare as he said, "Look, Tracy, it's been a very long day. What do you want?"

She cocked her head and fluttered her eyelids slightly. "Well, I was wondering if we could postpone our progress meeting tomorrow? I need a bit more time to get my report in order. I was thinking maybe I could get it to you maybe Monday next week?"

Mike frowned. So far Tracy had postponed their latest progress meeting three times, never giving a reason. "Tracy," he started with a slight sigh, "I know you work really hard on your research—"

He was about to point out to her that a PhD required more than just doing the actual research when she blurted out, "Thanks, I knew you'd understand." She dashed off without so much as a wave.

Mike gave a heavy sigh and shook his head. When was he going to learn? He started to wonder how much Tracy actually took advantage of him. Maybe she was just used to always getting her own way or she might even just not think about what she was doing half the time and spend the other half the time just thinking about having fun. Maybe he should take a leaf out of her book. That probably was his trouble; he thought too much.

There was little point chasing after her and, besides, if she didn't want to meet up that gave him more time for his own research, so he headed over to the staircase and started to ascend. He often wondered whose perverted sense of humour had arranged for his office to be on the fourth floor when all of his lectures were in the ground floor lecture theatre. In some ways he only had himself to blame as he'd promised himself he'd only use the stairs and avoid the lift in order to lose some of the puppy fat he was convinced his genes had saddled him with. So far it hadn't worked but he was determined to avoid spending money on a gym membership for as long as possible.

He reached the top of the stairs and turned left to go through a set of double doors that had a large red sign above them, baring the legend 'Physics Research Department' in large embossed silvery lettering. Since Teesside University was one of the recently converted polytechnic colleges, it didn't have as many departments as the older red-brick universities. Still, it was expanding and the School of Science and Technology now finally had departments of maths, computing, biology, chemistry and physics. It may still have had problems funding some of its research but at least it had decent offices, even if a number of the labs needed some work.

Secretly, Mike was really proud of the fact that he had his own office. He knew it was a luxury few people had these days, but he tried not to let it go to his head. He unlocked the third door on the left numbered 403 and tossed his notes on the small table by the door that he used for tutorials. He flicked his wrist and the door closed behind him and locked itself. He then snapped his fingers and the lights switched themselves on. Walking round to the other side of his desk, he half contemplated logging onto his computer and carrying on with his latest paper but decided he'd done enough for the day already. He raised his arms and his leather jacket rose off the back of his chair and fitted itself over his shoulders. He then raised his left arm and his shoulder bag rose off the floor and the strap flapped itself over his left shoulder. He put his laptop into the bag before heading out.

He got as far as the door when the phone rang on his desk. At first, he wondered if it was Cookey wanting to know when those exam papers would be ready, but then remembered that he was still in the US. He seriously considered letting it ring but his better nature won over and he reluctantly walked back and lifted the receiver into his hand with his will before holding it to his face. "Hello, Dr Michael Walker speaking."

"Yes, hello, Dr Walker." The voice was brisk, professional and female. "This is Detective Sergeant Granger from Middlesbrough CID."

Mike paused for a moment. Okay, this wasn't good. "Oh, uh, hello, yes, how can I help you, officer?"

"Do you know a young lady named Kerry Jones?"

Mike thought for a moment then realisation dawned on him. "Uh, yeah, I believe one of my first-year undergraduates is called that. Why do you ask?"

"Sir, could you possibly come over to Middlesbrough Police Station please?"

Chapter 3

"Sir?" Mike just stared. "Sir?"

He sighed. "Yeah, it's her."

Sergeant Jennifer Granger nodded to the pathologist who proceeded to pull the sheet over the corpse's face. "Would you like a drink of water, sir?"

"No, thank you. Is this the work of...?"

"Please, sir, I'd appreciate it if you didn't use that name around here. But yes, we believe so."

Mike looked at her slightly surprised. "I was going to say, 'that freak in the papers'."

Sergeant Granger sighed. "I'm sorry, sir. It's just not been a good week for us."

Mike looked over at the sheet covering the lifeless body. "Yeah I imagine it hasn't."

"Would you mind coming upstairs and giving us a statement please, sir?"

"Of course not. Lead the way." They headed out of the lab toward the small lift. "Actually," Mike suddenly said, "Could I possibly get that glass of water please?"

The young sergeant smiled. "Of course, sir. I'll get it for you upstairs."

She had quite a pretty face, Mike supposed, but her features were strong as if she was expressing outwardly how tough she was on the inside. She had kind eyes, though; they were light blue and her short blonde bob framed the whole effect quite nicely. Her attire of a white polo-neck jumper and dark slacks made her look casual enough for people to be comfortable around her, but professional enough to make someone think twice about messing with her. Mike had a strong feeling that it would be in his best interests to try and keep on her good side.

He found himself staring at the floor as they rode up in the lift. He hadn't felt this numb in a long time. He hardly knew the girl but still, she was one of his students. He had power, he should have been able to protect her, but he couldn't protect all the others in the papers. He hadn't even given them a thought. Sure, he'd been shocked like everyone else had when the killings had started and he'd become that little bit more cautious, even added a couple of extra wards to his house and office, but he hadn't thought about finding the monster himself. After all, why should he? It wasn't his problem. He wasn't a keeper, he was a seeker. God what was he thinking? He was neither now.

The lift took them to the seventh floor into a large open-plan office. The floor was packed with people and Mike couldn't help but notice that most of them looked either flustered, depressed or just plain angry. He suddenly felt a bit nervous. He'd never been very good with crowds, especially ones that looked angry and baying for blood; they always made him think back to his days of studying vampires. A chill ran down his spine and pain spiked across his back. He shook himself down and hoped that if anyone saw him, they just assumed he was thinking of Mad Jack. It was then that she ran into him.

"Oh, I'm sorry..." he started. The tiny figure had long, curly brown hair and a sharp, pretty face.

Unfortunately, it currently had an incredibly bad scowl spread across it, which spoilt things. She barely glanced up at him and carried on as if he hadn't even been there. *Story of my life*, Mike thought as he watched her head into the lift.

"Sorry about that, sir." Mike turned round to see a young man about his own age and height standing next to Sergeant Granger. "She's in a bit of a mood with me. Oh, sorry, where are my manners? I'm Detective Inspector David Walsh."

"Hello, Inspector. I'm Dr Michael Walker." Mike shook the man's outstretched hand and felt a sudden surge of energy spike up his arm and directly into his brain. Damn, he'd forgotten to put his guard up. One of the problems with being psychic was that physical touch caused transfer of intense emotions if you weren't properly prepared. Mike wasn't prepared and the inspector's feelings were certainly intense. He didn't get a direct look into the man's mind, but he did feel incredibly strong negative emotions; it was intense frustration mixed with a volatile rage. An intensely potent combination and Mike found himself stumbling slightly.

"Are you okay, sir?" the inspector asked as he grabbed Mike's shoulder.

Mike tried to pull himself together and ignore the sharp pain in his back. "Uh, I'm fine, thanks. Sorry. Uh, just thinking of Kerry, you know?"

The inspector gave him a suspicious look before continuing, "If you'll just follow me, please."

They entered a small room located at the back of the office. It contained a small rectangular table and four chairs. Inspector Walsh gestured Mike to take a seat and sat himself in one of the chairs on the opposite side of the table before placing a pad of paper in front of himself. Almost immediately, Sergeant Granger followed them in and placed a plastic cup filled with water in front of Mike before sitting down next to her superior.

Mike thanked her and took a quick swig of the water before looking back over at the two officers. "I'm afraid I've never done one of these before. Uh, what do you need me to do?"

"Oh, nothing much, sir," the inspector replied. "We'll ask you a series of questions and make notes, then we'll write it out as a statement, give it to you to read and then you can sign it."

"Uh, as long as you're happy with it, of course, sir," Sergeant Granger finished.

Mike couldn't help notice the inspector give her the eye and that she then flinched slightly. He was no expert on things like body language, but he didn't need his psychic power to tell him what that meant and he tried to suppress a smile.

He spent the next hour telling the two police officers what little he knew about Kerry. He explained to them that he barely knew her at all. She was one of his personal tutor group, which meant that he met her and two other first-year undergraduate students once a week to discuss their progress. He also told the two officers how he wasn't giving any first-year lectures that year and that she wasn't in any of his subject tutorial groups, which he met with every week to go through example exercises. Other than that, he didn't have much to tell them, except that he thought Kerry seemed to be a good kid who got quite good grades in her chosen subject.

"If you don't mind me asking, what do you lecture, sir?"

The inspector's question caught Mike off guard slightly. He wondered later if that was deliberate. "Oh, mainly maths, quantum physics and electronics."

"Interesting combination," the sergeant remarked. "What's your research interest, if you don't mind me asking, sir?"

Mike squirmed slightly. "Oh, I'm looking into new mathematical models of string theory."

"Hmm, sounds very complicated."

Mike had heard the inspector's attitude before; it was the one employed by people who pretended to be interested in science when in reality they couldn't give a toss about it. He always dealt with it in the same way – he ignored it.

Eventually, the inspector decided they had enough information and told Sergeant Granger to write up Mike's statement. While she did that, the inspector leaned back in his chair and stared at Mike intently, almost as if he was searching for something in Mike's face. It made Mike feel somewhat uncomfortable. "Is there something else you'd like to know, Inspector?"

Walsh leaned forward before responding, "I'm just curious, sir. Do you always dress this way?"

Mike smiled. "I'm strictly a tee shirt and jeans man, Inspector. And yes, some of my colleagues do say I look much more like a student than a member of staff but I choose to ignore them."

"I can appreciate that, sir, however, no offence, but don't you think that the leather jacket and trainers are a bit much?"

Mike was about to ask how a young police inspector was able to afford what looked to him like an Italian designer suit when the sergeant asked him to review his statement. Thanks to his marking experience, it didn't take him long to confirm that what she'd written was what he'd said, so he signed and dated the form. The inspector accepted it with what Mike was starting to feel was an increasingly suspicious look. It was making him feel more and more uncomfortable. The longer he was in Walsh's presence, the more Mike wanted to be out of it and he'd hoped that as soon as the statement was done, he could leave, but the inspector and Sergeant Granger remained firmly seated and silent.

Mike shuffled uncomfortably until finally he decided to break the ice. "Um, is there anything else, Inspector, or can I leave now?"

"That depends, sir."

Mike's eyes narrowed. "On what?"

"On whether there's anything else you want to tell us?"

Mike took a deep breath; he was really starting to hate this guy. "No, I've told you everything." He pushed the plain plastic chair away from the table with a horrible screeching sound and stood up. "Now, if you don't mind, I think I'd like to get home."

It was then that Sergeant Granger finally spoke. "Um, we may need to be in touch with you again, sir."

Mike produced one of his business cards from his jacket pocket and tossed it onto the table. "All of my contact details are on here. I haven't got any business trips or holidays planned."

"Keep it that way, sir," Walsh said almost slyly.

Mike said nothing more but made sure he gave the inspector a dirty look as he left.

Mike stomped out of the lift in frustration. His exposure to the police had been primarily through books and television shows but he was starting to wonder if some of the stereotypes about them might just be true after all. They'd certainly tried the good cop, bad cop routine on him. Or at least he hoped that they were just trying it on. The thought of anyone, even an idiot like that inspector, thinking that he could possibly have something to do with Kerry's death made his blood boil. He tried to keep his temper under control but he still felt a slight sharp pain in his back, so he stood by the lift for a moment to catch his breath and get his emotions under control.

It was just as he was heading toward the door that he saw the couple standing by the desk. The man looked to be in his mid to late fifties and about five foot nine. He had a heavy face in every sense of the word. His features were strong but his eyes showed all the signs of fatigue brought about by being woken from slumber prematurely or suffering from an incredible amount of stress. His face looked familiar to Mike, but he couldn't quite place it until the woman next to him stood up from signing the visitors' book. Her long, curly black hair fell away from her face, showing that she too was approaching 50 from the wrong direction, but she was still attractive, even now with her clearly tear-reddened eyes. It wasn't difficult for Mike to realise who she was; the resemblance to her daughter was uncanny.

He walked up to them as they approached the lift. "Uh, Mr and Mrs Jones?" The woman just looked at him with eyes that looked hollow and empty but the man nodded. "Sorry, uh, my name is Dr Michael Walker." A confused look followed by a small amount of realisation came over the couple's eyes and they both looked at him more closely. "I, um, that is... I just wanted to say... I'm just so sorry." Kerry's father nodded stiffly but her mother burst into tears.

Mike stood to one side and let them pass, instantly regretting opening his big mouth. It was then that he noticed Sergeant Granger coming out of the lift to meet them. Not wanting to be anywhere near her or the other copper, he turned around and dashed out of the building. He realised that he'd just been the one who'd killed the last bit of hope those poor parents had that their beloved daughter was okay and that this had all been some sort of sick joke or a terrible mistake. His stomach started to feel like it was tying itself into a knot as he stepped through the doors into the outside world.

The darkness of the late night had descended while he'd been in the station. A three-quarter moon shone clearly and the few stars bright enough to overcome the town's light pollution pierced the black sky like tiny pinpricks of hope in the seemingly endless void of space.

Mike was somewhat surprised to find two uniformed policemen were now guarding the glass double doors of the station like sentinels. They were tall, stocky and imposing, and both gave Mike a sombre nod as he left. It was only as he reached the bottom of the half a dozen steps that led back down to street level that he realised what they were there for. Almost immediately after taking the last step, a small group of people of various sizes, shapes and gender, who had been loitering disconnectedly around the base of the steps, suddenly all dashed toward him and congregated around him. Some started brandishing business cards, others held dictaphones or snapped his picture with cameras or their mobile phones and some even used old-fashion notebooks and pens, ready to scribble his every word as they bombarded him with a sudden assault of questions.

"Excuse me, sir, are you Dr Michael Walker?"

How on Earth did they get his name?

"Is it true that the latest victim was one of your students, sir?"

'Was'. Yeah, she most definitely 'was'. 'Was' now being the operative word. Bloody vultures, did they even care about that?

He pushed his way through the throng of reporters trying hard not to make eye contact with any of them. They expertly left him just enough room to squeeze through but still remained close enough to keep bombarding him with questions.

"Have you seen her body?"

"Can you say what he did to her?"

"Do you have any comment to make?"

After he was through the last of them, Mike turned round and ever so slightly flexed his fingers before saying, "I have no comment to make, now please leave me alone!" And they did, though most of them didn't know why they did. Satisfied that the spell had worked, Mike turned around and continued on to his car.

The university's car park was located on Southfield Road, only five minutes' walk away from the police station, so Mike was soon entering the private multistorey and none too soon, as far as he was concerned. He wanted to get as far away from that damn police station and its inhabitants as soon as possible.

He almost felt physically ill from the guilt of what he'd said to Kerry's poor parents. It was just so wrong. She was a good student and she had so much to live for and even if she wasn't, her family didn't deserve all this suffering, it was so wrong.

His small silver Ford Focus was the last vehicle remaining in the car park when he finally got to it. He reached the car door with his key ready and was just about to press the radio button to unlock it when he stopped, swore under his breath, turned around and went back the way he came.

Chapter 4

Mike headed out of the car park and left the university grounds. He walked up to the next street and then turned the corner and headed toward the old row of terraced buildings that were tucked away in the next street behind the offices of the *Evening Gazette*. To the casual observer the building looked like nothing more than any of the many others in the old town. It was a large, whitewashed structure and like most in Middlesbrough, it was no taller than three stories. A small and barely noticeable gold plaque next to the door bore the inscription 'Order Of The Cunning Ones' in black stencilled letters. Of course, most people who looked at it couldn't see that.

He stood outside for a moment and wondered what the hell he was doing there. He wasn't going to be warmly welcomed, that was for sure, and what exactly did he expect to find? Answers? The reason he'd left in the first place was to look for those! Then again, he was looking for a different truth now.

He reached into the inside pocket of his leather jacket and pulled on a slim silver chain that proceeded to slither out of his coat like a thin shiny worm, bringing with it a small silver disc about two centimetres in diameter. He held up the talisman and watched it spin round, alternating between its two symbols; a sword enclosed within a ring made up of 12 points on one side and a six-point star on the other. He'd often wondered why he kept carrying the damn thing around with him. It wasn't like he needed reminding of his past or that he worried about losing the stupid thing, but now he was actually glad that he had it with him, or at least he thought he was.

Oh, to hell with it. He placed the chain over his head and pushed the large heavy door open. He felt the amulet part the powerful energy of the protective wards like a stage curtain as he walked through.

The entrance hall was just as he remembered it, with its plush red carpet, oak trim, long corridors, solid oak doors, an ornate staircase and lime green walls that were covered in expensive-looking paintings. It even smelt exactly the same, that same strong lemony scent as if the place had constantly just been cleaned. Mike had always thought the place looked like an old-fashioned gentlemen's club and it seemed to be just as resistant to change.

The painting on the wall nearest to him showed a tall, thin man with a balding head and a ridiculously large white handlebar moustache, wearing an immaculately pressed three-piece suit. As Mike's eyes were drawn toward it, the image began to shimmer and the man's features started to gently contort in a fluid-like motion as if they were waves on the sea. His face started to extend out of the picture, followed by his body, his arms and finally his legs. They did not appear solid though, they were transparent and ghost-like.

The man glided down to the floor and stood to attention in front of Mike before bowing slightly. "Good evening, sir," he said in an extremely polite Queen's English. "How may I help you?"

Mike paused for a moment, wondering what to say. How could he help him? What was he here for? He sighed; there was only really one option. "Could I possibly speak to Vice-Mage Saban, please?"

"I shall see if he is available, sir. Am I correct in saying that it is Mr Michael Walker calling?"

"No, it's Dr Michael Walker calling!" He wasn't too concerned about sounding rude; the butler was nothing more than an automaton, effectively an elaborate answering machine and he was damned if he was going to let Chris or any of the rest of them think that the title he'd earned in his years away meant nothing.

"Very good, sir. If you wouldn't mind waiting here." With that, the butler-like spectral image faded into thin air.

Mike whistled through his teeth and shuffled around awkwardly, wondering again what the hell he was thinking he'd achieve by coming here. He'd just turned around and faced the door when he heard the voice behind him. "Well, well, well, look what the cat dragged in."

Mike turned back around, looked up to the top of the staircase and gave a heavy sigh. "Hello, Jon, how have you been?"

Jonathon Rawlins was standing at the top of the stairs holding a jet-black cane with a round silver handle in his left hand. He looked down at Mike with disdain. Mike was trying hard to return the look with equal dislike, but having never been very good at facial expressions, he was sure he failed. "I assume you have a good reason for being here?" Jon asked, ignoring Mike's fake attempt at polite conversation.

Mike considered keeping up the pretext of being civil for about half a second, then replied, "Not that it's any of your business but I'm here to see Chris."

The eyes on Jon's perfectly symmetrical handsome face narrowed and fixed Mike with a cold stare. Mike had always hated that face; it was everything his own wasn't – narrow instead of round, a perfect chin (no cleft), full head of curly hair (not receding). The list went on and he supposed it was one of the reasons the two of them had never got on ever since they met all those years ago at the Academy. Mike tried hard not to let himself get wound up; he knew that would be exactly what Jon wanted. So there they stood like two overgrown schoolboys, staring each other down.

Eventually Jon started to descend the staircase, slowly and deliberately, the long flowing black robes with silver trim that he wore to identify himself as a keeper of the Order flapping around his expensive-looking jet-black shirt and slacks like a living shadow as he approached. "And what," Jon asked, "does the vice-mage of our Chapter want with you?"

"He doesn't want anything with me," Mike replied coolly. "I want to speak to him and before you ask, it's none of your business."

Jon had reached the foot of the stairs by then and stood toe to toe with Mike. Although he was by no means short at five foot eleven, Mike had always felt a bit dwarfed by Jon's six-foot-three frame. Yet another reason they didn't get on. Jon raised the cane and transferred it to his right hand before pointing the tip at Mike menacingly, barely a centimetre from his nose. "Anything you do is my business, Michael Walker."

"Oh, and why is that, Jonathon Rawlins? Because you're a keeper?"

"Not just any keeper," Jon stated firmly with menace in his eyes and Mike fought the urge to rub his back. Jon lowered the cane but didn't relax. "I'll ask you again; why are you here?"

"I already told you; to see Chris."

Jon's face went red. "That's Vice-Mage Saban to you!"

"I was his apprentice for five years; I think I can call him by his first name. What's the matter, Jonny, still haven't earned that little privilege?"

The wizard bared his teeth and raised his cane again. "Now you listen to me, you son of a—"

"Ahem." The nervous little cough came from a nervous little man with a balding head and glasses, who'd just appeared beside them. Everything about him was brown, from the light brown tweed suit he wore, complete with brown shirt and tie to even his robes. They all seemed to match his eye colour as well as what was left of his hair. The whole effect made Mike think that he looked like a businessman from the seventies. The image was spoilt only slightly by the four-foot length of timber he was holding in his left hand. "Is there a problem, Keeper Rawlins?" the little man asked nervously.

"Oh no. No trouble at all," Mike piped in before Jon had a chance to speak. "Jon and I are old friends; we went to the Academy together and were just catching up on old times. Isn't that right, Jonny?" Jon was silent. Mike beamed a smile at the keeper and turned back to the man in brown. "Sorry, I don't believe we've met, Mr...?"

The man shuffled nervously and gave a slight smile. "Oh, uh, Simpkins, sir. Peter Simpkins." He extended his hand, which Mike shook warmly. "Treasurer of the Teesside Chapter of the Order Of The Cunning Ones."

"Michael Walker," Mike replied, being sure to keep his psychic defences up this time.

Peter Simpkins's eyes lit up, a reaction that certainly surprised Mike. "Ah, I've been looking for you, sir. Vice-Mage Saban would like you to join him in his office."

"Excellent, please lead the way." Mike gave Jon his best victory grin and said a cheerful, "I'll catch you later, Jonny." As he followed Simpkins, he could see his old classmate's scowl.

The treasurer led him through a complex series of corridors and staircases before stopping in front of one of the many identical-looking solid oak doors that seemed to line every wall at regular intervals. Simpkins knocked on it three times with the simple wooden staff he was carrying and the door automatically unlocked itself and swung open. Simpkins stood to one side and gestured for Mike to go inside. "Aren't you joining us?" Mike asked.

"Oh, the vice-mage's office is not a place for someone of my level when I'm not invited, sir. Have a nice day." With that, he muttered a single word under his breath and vanished in a puff of smoke. Mike shook his head and walked through the door. He couldn't believe that weird little fellow was still using an old spell like that in this day and age.

He stood in the doorway for a few moments and looked around the room. It was certainly a study all right, filled from top to bottom with shelves full of books. Mike was pretty sure they were all Grimoires, or spell books as some people liked to call them.

The air in the room was thick with the smell of old paper and a mild hint of cinnamon – no doubt Chris still had a thing for incense sticks in his spells. The only light appeared to come from a huge stained-glass window at the back; it depicted a man wearing long flowing blue robes and holding a huge wooden staff. One of the many effigies to the founder of the Order that were found in all the Chapters.

"Well?"

Mike tore his gaze away from the window and looked down at the man sitting at the expensive mahogany desk in front of it. He was in his early sixties, with curly white hair and a strong face. The type who would have been a looker in his youth, real popular with the ladies. Now his features were heavy with age and his figure rounded out. He was dressed in a more modern and, in Mike's opinion, sharper-looking business suit than the one Peter Simpkins wore and it was set off by black robes like Jon's, but with gold trim instead of silver. Christopher Saban, vice-mage of the Teesside Chapter of the Order Of The Cunning Ones, the most powerful Order of wizards in Britain and possibly the world, looked up at his old apprentice slowly and gave a wry smile.

Mike took two steps toward the desk and the door swung shut behind him and locked itself. He stopped suddenly and looked back at it briefly before returning his attention once more to his old master. Chris grinned. "I wouldn't want us to be disturbed."

Mike snorted slightly and stood in front of the desk. He looked around. "Are you always this courteous to your guests, Chris?"

The vice-mage snickered slightly. "Oh, I am sorry, Michael. I almost forgot." He reached under his desk and produced a six-foot-long staff made of solid oak with a large red orb burnt into one end. He waved it in the air and the orb glowed brightly. Suddenly, thousands of small, thin pieces of wood, no bigger than toothpicks, started to splinter off all the bookshelves. They twisted and spun around together like a swarm of locusts, then they gathered together in a massive lump, before starting to meld into each other and slowly take on a new shape. Then, with a flash of light, they had fully materialised into a small chair and dropped to the floor in front of Mike next to the vice-mage's desk. Chris smiled at his former apprentice and gestured to it. "Please be seated."

Mike looked at the ridiculously small seat and felt almost disgusted. It was barely big enough for a five-year-old, but he nodded politely and said, "Thank you." Gingerly sitting down. The vice-mage stared at him across his desk. Mike decided he'd better break the ice. "I suppose congratulations are in order, Vice-Mage Saban."

Chris smiled at him; he was one of the few people Mike knew who could put on a smile without any warmth in it. "Thank you, Michael, I must say I was disappointed that you couldn't make my inauguration ceremony."

"I'll bet you were."

"So, what can I do for you, my former apprentice? Would you like to rejoin our Order? Your knowledge of magic would be of great use to us. I'm sure I could put in a good word for you with the arch-mage..."

"Uh, no thank you, Chris. I think we both know that wouldn't be possible." Mike rubbed his back and Chris gave him that same cold smile.

"Yes, that's true. So, if that's not it, then what, may I ask, is your reason for visiting?"

Mike took a deep breath; it was now or never. "I need help."

"Oh really? What sort of help?"

"I need a spell to find someone. One that doesn't require a personal possession."

"There is no such spell."

"Oh, come on. You're telling me that in all your years of researching the Arts, you've never come across any alternative ways of scrying!"

"There are thousands of ways of scrying, Michael. You can use circles, crystal balls even familiars to find someone but they all have one thing in common; they all require a personal item."

Mike was silent for a minute; he really wished he wasn't expecting that but, in his heart, he knew it was true. "Okay then, what about some way of, I don't know, putting a trace on someone, marking them with something so that you can scry for them without them knowing it?"

"Why would you want to do such a thing?" Chris' tone was completely neutral, but Mike could tell he was suspicious by the way the old man's left eyebrow twitched slightly.

Mike sighed again and considered his next move. He had thought of a number of different lies to tell Chris but had discounted all of them as being simply too ridiculous to possibly be believed. In the end, he decided the only thing that he could try was the truth. "Do you read the papers?" he asked as calmly as he could.

"Of course."

"Then you know about the serial killer, Mad Jack?" Chris was silent so he went on. "He killed one of my students yesterday." Still silence. "I want to find him and stop him." Still more silence. "Come on, Chris, there must be something we can do. All this power, all this knowledge and we..."

"We keep the Code."

"We have knowledge that could help people, save people."

"And we protect people when that knowledge is abused."

"And that's all we do? We just bury our heads in the sand and let people suffer? I've had enough, Chris, I'm sick of hiding!" Silence fell. Mike was even shocked at himself for saying it.

Chris slowly leaned across the desk and stared at his former apprentice. "For your sake, I'll pretend I didn't hear that, but I warn you, you're going down a dangerous road, Michael. You're not the first to question our ways and though I'm sure you won't be the last, just remember that life is this way for a reason."

Mike had calmed down a bit but was still mad enough to find himself saying, "So we just let people die..."

"Shit happens, Michael. Get over it. Just remember, if ever you get ideas about revealing the truth, well..."

"I'll have a visit from the keepers."

"I hope it doesn't come to that, Michael."

"And what about all the people that this nut's killed? And, more importantly, what about all the others he's going to kill? You know what, Chris, you're all just as much of a monster as he is!"

Chris slammed his hand on the desk, causing a noise like a huge clap of thunder to echo around the room. It ripped through Mike's ears and he jumped slightly. "That will do, Michael. This conversation is over!" Mike found himself breathing heavily. "I suggest that you leave now!"

Mike sat there for a few moments but finally caught his breath and managed to mutter, "Thanks for nothing, Chris." With that, he stood up and stormed out.

Chapter 5

Amy had arrived back at the Teesside offices of the Crown Prosecution Service in a foul mood; she really was getting sick of Dave treating her like a child. She hated being the youngest; everyone thought that they had the right to boss her around and tell her what she could and couldn't do. Well, she was going to show them. This was her chance to shine and she was damned if she was going to let Dave or anyone else get in her way. She was just about to enter the horrible old square-shaped building when there was a tap on her shoulder. Her heart sank when she turned around. Could this day possibly get any worse?

"Hi, Amy. Did you miss me?"

Her frown indicated that she hadn't. "What do you want, Kev?"

Kevin Turner gave his ex-girlfriend a wide smile. "Can't I still care about you enough to see how you are? It's really great to see you back in town, by the way, after all this time."

"I've only been gone for three years while I got my PhD."

"Really? It seems so much longer. How have you been keeping?"

"Cut the crap, Kev. Shouldn't you be parked outside the police station with the other hacks waiting for someone to pounce on? I assume you're still writing half-true stories for the local rag?"

He gave a slight smirk on his narrow face and rubbed a hand through his thick, greasy black hair. At five-foot-three he was short for a guy but was still a couple of inches taller than her petite five-foot-one frame. It had been one of the things that had once attracted her to him; she had thought he looked like a cute kid. Now with his messy dark hair, piercing green eyes and narrow face, she thought he looked more like a certain type of vermin you found in sewers.

Kev appeared not to notice her indifference to his presence and carried on almost like they were still together. "Well, I wasn't going to bring it up but since you asked, Amy, I was wondering if you'd just come back from seeing your brother?"

"No comment, Kev." With that, she turned her back on him and continued on into the CPS.

"Oh, come on, Amy, give me something…"

She didn't hear the rest of his reply as she left him talking to the revolving entrance door. Rushing through the building to her office, she wondered what had ever possessed her to date a journalism student who wanted to be a reporter in the first place.

Like most criminologists, Amy was self-employed but used a consultancy service called the Psychological Behavioural Agency, or PBA, as it was known for short, to find work for her. She'd signed on with the PBA as soon as she got her PhD but had been more or less sat twiddling her thumbs for the last three months. The majority of her peers worked mainly in the south-east near London but Amy had the bright idea to make her hometown in the north-east of England her base of operations. This would enable her to provide services to the local authorities there to effectively fill what she saw as a gap in the market. At first this seemed like a disaster with her only getting small jobs helping out other consultants but then the Mad Jack case came up and since many of her peers were already knee-deep in other work, she'd managed to persuade the agency to let her do the initial psychological profile.

Unfortunately, that meant that she currently had no office of her own and her darling brother had made it perfectly clear that there was no space for her to bunk in Middlesbrough CID or anywhere else in his precious police station to get properly involved with the investigation. Fortunately, or possibly unfortunately, for Amy, the prosecutor for the Mad Jack case had already been assigned so that when the lunatic was brought to justice, the evidence was already halfway organised for trial. That prosecutor was Emma Walsh, one of the lead barristers for the violent crime section of Teesside CPS. She was also Amy and Dave's older sister!

Although Emma had a reputation as a hard-nosed prosecutor, who was known to bully anyone who worked for or with her, including the solicitors who prepared her cases, she had been more than willing to let Amy share an office with her lead solicitor, Thomas Grier, on the condition that Amy kept her informed on the progress of the investigation. The plus side of this was that Amy enjoyed the benefits of having a proper desk, including her own computer and chair. The disadvantage was that said office was attached directly to Emma's. Hence Amy found herself at the constant beck and call of her sister's demands, even though she technically didn't work for her at all. Amy had always known that Emma had an almost obsessive curiosity about how police investigated her cases but she had never anticipated Emma would expect Amy be her spy in the camp and report all aspects of the Mad Jack investigation back to her, whether Amy like it or not!

There was a positive for Amy, though; she got on very well with Thomas, or Tom, as she liked to call him. He'd always made her feel welcome even though she was effectively invading his space and they shared the same cheeky sense of humour. Amy couldn't help but think that he was more than a little relieved to find out that she was nothing like her sister!

Tom was in his usual position behind his desk reviewing documents when she entered. He was quite a tall man, just over six feet in height, with short, jet-black curly hair. He had a smooth round face that was permanently set off by a pair of thick black glasses. On someone else they would have probably looked goofy, but Amy had always thought they made him look sophisticated – the fact that he was always impeccably dressed probably helped as well. Although he was clearly deeply involved in what he was reading, he still made the time to look up and smile when Amy walked in. "Hi, Amy," he chirped cheerfully, "Sergeant Granger's sent the reports you wanted over. They're on your desk."

Amy sighed slightly and smiled. "Thanks, Tom. You're a star."

"I wouldn't sit down if I were you. Emma wanted to see you in her office as soon as you got back."

Amy found herself sighing again. "Thanks."

She hung her coat up on the stand by Tom's desk before going over to the other side of the room to knock on the connecting door that joined the senior barrister's office to theirs. She waited for the matriarchal authoritative voice to give her permission to enter before she did so. Emma was a formidable-looking woman in every sense of the word. Like Amy, she was slim with a thick mane of curly black hair but, unlike Amy, she constantly had a stern look about her. Some had said that she could make a grown man wilt with merely a furtive glance. She was currently sitting behind her desk with the receiver of her desk phone pressed firmly against her left ear.

She beckoned Amy in and gestured her to a seat before covering the mouthpiece with her right hand. "I won't be a minute." She then removed her hand and returned to the call. "Now you listen to me, Paul, I do not give a shit about that. I want him in court first thing tomorrow morning."

Amy sat uncomfortably for what seemed to her more like 10 minutes and tried to fight the growing urge to squirm in her seat. Finally, Emma replaced the receiver on the phone and turned her attention to her sister. "So, how did it go?" she asked simply. That was the defining characteristic of Emma Walsh – straight to the point and not interested in anything else. No small talk, no banter. Just business. Even with family.

"Oh, very well," was Amy's reply. She knew she was stretching the truth and trying to be more than a little diplomatic but she didn't want Emma thinking that their 'source' in the police wasn't as helpful as she'd made them out to be.

"So Dave didn't give you any trouble?" Amy just shook her head. "Good," Emma said. Thank God she seemed to have bought it. "So when do you think you'll have your profile ready?"

"Well, it could take a while. You see I have to digest all the information from the police, which I'm sure you realise can take a lot of time…"

"Try to take less."

"Uh, yes. I'll try, uh, I mean, I will. You see, Emma, I've got to—"

"You know how important this is, Amy," Emma said, cutting her off. "This investigation could show real co-operation between the CPS and local police and the mayor's going to be watching us. There's already been six victims now and I want to see this lunatic in the dock before we get to number seven. That's why I've been pestering those idiots in Middlesbrough's finest to get a professional criminal profiler onboard, but they've been stonewalling me at every turn. It was only by threatening to get the mayor involved that I was able to persuade them to use your skills."

"Yes, I understand that and believe me, Emma, I really appreciate what you've done for me and I certainly want to catch this bastard as much as everyone else."

"Good, then go get to work."

Amy gulped then nodded nervously and excused herself. Just as she reached the door she turned back to the barrister. "Uh, Emma?"

"Yes?"

"Um, I do appreciate that you've let me stay with you and Tom, but um… Well, I think I can work on the profile better if I work from home for the next few days."

Emma gave her a sceptical look for a minute but eventually said, "Fine. Just get it done quickly."

"Will do." With that, she left.

Tom waited until Amy closed the door and had sat down at her desk before asking the question, "So how did it go?"

"Do you mean with Emma or down the station?"

"Both."

"With Emma, fine, I suppose."

"But not with your brother?"

"He wasn't exactly willing to share information." At this point she held up one of the files that had magically appeared on her desk while she was out. "Thankfully, his sergeant is being a little more co-operative."

"Probably their superiors had some influence over it."

"True."

Tom pushed his thick black glasses up off the ridge of his nose and gave a sigh of his own. His round face took on a strange heavy look that Amy had never seen before. "Look, honey, you know I don't often go all gung-ho but I just want to let you know that I think what you're doing is a really great thing. The police need all the help they can get stopping this nut and if there's anything I can do to help, please just ask."

Amy smiled. "Thanks, Tom."

"No worries. I've gotta say, I hope that this works. Right now, it seems like they need a miracle to catch this guy."

"A miracle? Tom, we need a magician!"

Chapter 6

Mike wrote the last symbol in the air with his index finger and took a step back to look at the ghostly black writing as it shimmered, suspended in mid-air. One of the great advantages of being a sorcerer was that he didn't need to invest in a whiteboard and marker pens for his own research at home. He snapped his fingers at the laptop in the corner of the room and the Dictaphone program started running.

"Okay, experimental theorem number two eight seven. If the power contained within the circle is directly proportional to two pi r..." He stopped and grumbled under his breath, "Damn it. That should be pi r squared." He rubbed his hand over the offending formula and the writing shimmered into thin air. He then proceeded to write the correct expression in its place. "OK, the circle contains the energy directly proportional to pi r squared. If that's true, then..." He sighed. "Shit. It's no good." He snapped his fingers again and the laptop program shut down. He then swiped his arm over the whole equation and it faded away to nothing.

Try as he might, he just couldn't concentrate. He found himself pacing around the room for a few minutes before making his way downstairs to the lounge. He needed to try and relax; maybe there was something good on the telly. He flopped into one of the soft two-seater settees and clicked his fingers at the flat screen television he kept in the corner of the room. The TV switched itself on with its usual click and BBC1 flickered to life.

"The latest victim has been confirmed tonight as 18-year-old student, Kerry Jones." Mike's eyes widened as he sat bolt upright. The reporter stood on a section of pavement that he immediately recognised. She swept her arm in a grand gesture toward a collection of small, bright lights in the darkness of the night somewhere in the distance and continued. "Her body was found here on Redcar beach in the early hours of this morning. The police are still—" Mike snapped his fingers again and the image and its associated sound vanished.

Redcar, the bastard had dumped Kerry on Redcar beach, barely a stone's throw away from his home! True, the modern housing estate he lived in was hardly on the seafront's doorstep, or even in the town centre, but still, Mad Jack had dumped her body near Mike's home, near where he lived! The sick freak had probably done it last night. He'd probably done it while Mike was fast asleep, all cosy in his nice, safe, comfortable bed. He'd just slept peacefully while poor Kerry had been... Damn it, what was his problem? He barely knew the girl and, as Chris had pointed out to him, there was nothing he could do for her now. God, he needed to get out of the house.

He jumped up and made a quick detour to the kitchen to pick up his car keys before grabbing his jacket off the banister and heading for the front door. After activating both his alarm and protective wards, he left the house, jumped into his car and drove off.

He found himself heading out of his housing estate and back toward Middlesbrough along the usual route he took to work. He wasn't quite sure where he was heading or what he was even doing. Maybe he was hoping that a random drive would just clear his head, but for some reason he found himself exiting the main road and taking the slip road to Marton, the middle-class suburb that he'd grown up in. It was only when he started to wonder what he was doing there that he noticed that he was parking the car in front of Saint Luke's Anglican Church. He sat there for a minute and sighed. Now he knew he was losing it.

In his conscious mind he decided to just drive away, but his body decided to get out of the car and walk toward the cemetery that was behind the main church building. Before he realised it, he found himself standing over the same grave that he visited every week and looking down at the tombstone. "So what do I do now?" He found himself asking it, but he got no reply.

Damn, it was freezing out here. He zipped up his jacket and stuffed his hands in his pockets. He stood there reading and rereading the inscription on the stone through the steam of his breath for what must have been 10 minutes. Eventually he had enough of torturing himself and turned away.

Now, as he walked out of the cemetery, he found himself heading into the church building itself. It wasn't one of those grand old structures that most people associated with the house of the Lord. In fact, it was a relatively new building that had been custom-built in the eighties at the same time as the shopping centre next door. Mike had always thought that from the outside its square, blocky shape and dirty brown bricks made it look somewhat like a throwback to the sixties style of brutalist architecture. Or at least what the sixties style of architecture would have looked like if they could afford bricks instead of just concrete!

He took out his key and unlocked the large wooden doors. They opened with a loud squeak as he entered. The inside of the church was a different story to the outside; the congregation area was a large, airy affair with plenty of pews and an effigy to the son of God hung at the front above a magnificent pulpit made of mahogany that stood proudly at the centre. On a Sunday, the hall was usually packed with parishioners, but tonight, it was silent.

Mike had always found that there was something amazing about the quietness of a church. Normally, total silence was eerie, but in churches it was just peaceful. Of course, the fact that his power was effectively switched off when he walked on holy ground helped with that.

He walked down to the front, sat on one of the benches near the congregation area and leaned his head forward in a silent prayer before looking up at the large cross hung above the pulpit and thought about all that it represented.

"So, what should I do? Huh?" Silence. Mike shook his head. "Yeah, I know. I've got no right asking you for advice."

"All can ask the Lord's advice."

Mike nearly jumped out of his skin. When he looked to his left, he found a short woman in her mid-fifties, with curly brown hair, standing next to him. Although she was wearing faded grey jeans and cowboy boots, she still had on the traditional black shirt and dog collar to identify herself as the church's vicar.

"Jesus, are you trying to scare me to death?"

The reverend's face went stony. "I'd appreciate it if you didn't use language like that here."

Mike went red. "Sorry."

She smiled and her face softened. "That's okay," she said as she sat herself down next to him. "I must say I'm surprised to see you here, Michael, especially at this time."

Mike sighed. "Yeah, well I'm not really sure why I'm here myself."

She took on a concerned look. "Are you okay?"

He shook his head. "Not really, no."

"Do you want to talk about it?"

He paused and tried to gather his thoughts. Did he want to talk about it? What was there to talk about? Eventually, he turned to the Vicar and asked, "You know about Mad Jack?"

She nodded. "Of course, terrible business."

"His latest victim, the one he killed yesterday? The one they found on Redcar beach near my house? Well, she was one of my students and I had to go and identify her this afternoon."

"Oh, Michael, I'm so sorry." She put her arm round him and rubbed his shoulder gently.

Mike shook his head again. "I mean, I barely knew her, but still…"

"You feel that you could have done something."

He nodded solemnly. "I sometimes think I can do so much more. I mean, the power I have…"

"You're not God, Michael."

"Tell me about it." He buried his face in his hands and started shaking his head once more.

The vicar paused for a moment to let him compose himself before she continued. "You can't solve every problem that happens in the world, Michael. In fact, weren't you the one who once told me that magic wasn't the be all and end all to the world's ills? I mean, wasn't that why you wanted to study science in the first place? After all, you were..." She stopped. Mike had suddenly looked up straight ahead and his mouth had dropped wide open. "Are you okay, Michael? What's wrong?"

He started to laugh. "Aw, man, how could I have been so stupid?" With that, he jumped up and ran toward the door. He was just about to open it when he stopped, turned around, dashed back, and kissed the vicar on her cheek. "Thanks, Mum," he said before running out toward his car. Sarah Walker just sat there and shook her head with a smile as her son left.

Chapter 7

Middlesbrough police force may not have been known for its glamour, but it was known for its efficiency; or at least that was what the management told its staff. Thus, when they had recently renovated CID's offices, they'd decided to save valuable space by making two officers share a single desk, with one seated on each of the sides, separated by an invisible line. Though this was usually limited to rookie constables, the Mad Jack investigation had required a special dedicated task force to be set up and that had meant more officers with fewer desks. Hence Dave and Jenny had both volunteered to share a desk with each other and they were both hoping that nobody noticed how eager they were to do so!

It was the chair on his side of that shared desk that Inspector David Walsh was slumping himself into now. Sergeant Jennifer Granger watched him over the new flat screen monitor that had recently been installed on her computer; the inspector looked like he was desperately trying to keep his cool. Jenny guessed that his debrief with Superintendent Shaw had not gone well and he was looking for somewhere to vent his frustration. She hoped that he wasn't still miffed that she'd had to go behind his back and give Amy the case files she'd wanted. It wasn't her fault that the superintendent had ordered her to hand them over!

Jenny watched Dave carefully with a strange feeling in her stomach; it wasn't fear, more of concern. "Sir?" She asked the question carefully as if trying to get his attention even though the way he was looking over at her seemed to indicate that she already had it. Eventually she decided to risk continuing. "Sir? Are you okay?"

He sighed and rubbed his face. "No, I'm not, Sergeant. We're getting nowhere fast."

Jenny found herself slouching as if she'd just been crushed by a heavy weight. "Did the super give you a hard time, sir?"

Dave shook his head. "Not exactly. He just reminded me again about how important it is to solve this case before anyone else dies. Like I didn't know that already." He leaned back and ran his fingers through his hair. "Let's go through it again from the very beginning." With that, he stood up and headed toward the whiteboard they kept at the back of the office.

Jenny fought back a sigh of her own. *Here we go again*, she thought. Why did he torture himself like this? Despite this opinion, she found herself saying, "Okay, sir." She stood up and followed him toward the board.

The inspector had fixed up two pictures of each of the victims in chronological order from left to right on the top of the whiteboard. One was a picture taken from when they were alive that had been provided by the family of the deceased; the other was one of the official photographs taken by the coroner as part of the autopsy procedure. Dave had told the entire team that it was so that they never forgot what they were there for. Namely to find the monster that had taken away the vibrant living person on the left and turned them into the horrifying image on the right. Underneath each pair of pictures, the victim's name had been written, along with the date of their death and where and when they were found in thick blue marker pen. It was literally a timeline of death. A timeline of Mad Jack.

Jenny and Dave stood in front of the board for a few minutes before Dave stabbed his finger on the very first picture, which showed the cheerful face of a middle-aged man with brown eyes and receding hair. "The first victim was John Talbot, a 52-year-old white male who owned his own used car business just outside the town centre. Despite the stereotype of people in his profession, he was apparently a decent upstanding member of the community who was liked by both friends and employees alike. He went missing after working late one night and never made it home. He was found a couple of days later floating in the River Tees." He paused for a moment as he looked at the autopsy photo that showed the multiple stab wounds that caused John Talbot's death. "He was married with two grown-up daughters and was about to become a grandfather for the first time."

Jenny nodded soberly and looked at the next two pairs of pictures. The first image of the first pair showed a fairly handsome man with spiky blonde hair and a cheesy grin, the first picture of the second pair showed a woman with her curly, jet-black hair blowing in the wind. Coupled with the amazing smile that she was wearing, she could have easily been a model, in Jenny's opinion. "The second and third victims were Steven and Anne Waverly," she found herself saying. "A couple in their early thirties who, from what we can gather, were out for a late-night walk in Stewart's Park. He was found the next morning by the park warden. She was found a few days later in virtually the same area of the park."

"Which meant that he killed and raped her somewhere else and brought her back to the park to dump her." Dave looked at her second photo. "After he'd done that to her."

Jenny nodded. The images of what the couple looked like after they were found almost made her shudder. The bastard had not only stabbed them repeatedly but slashed both their faces. Jenny looked over at Dave and continued. "He was an IT support engineer and she was a part-time singer. They'd been married for two years." Again, Jenny paused. "And she was two months pregnant!"

Dave closed his eyes for a moment, then carried on. "Okay, so after them, he starts to develop a pattern; killing and raping women then dumping their bodies a few days after taking them."

Jenny nodded again and looked at the fourth pair of photographs. The first one was of another middle-aged woman sat on a chair with a baby boy perched on her knee. The second picture of the pair showed her with the same stab wounds as the other victims. "Yeah, so far he's killed Diane Walder, a 34-year-old unemployed single mother who was found by the war memorial." She looked along to the fifth pair of photographs, those of a young blonde woman before and after Mad Jack met her. "Sarah Carter, a 27-year-old employee of Tesco who was found in the car park of the very store where she worked." Her eyes wandered along the grim line once more; the inspector had just put the sixth pair of photographs up on the board that very morning. "And now he's killed Kerry Jones, an 18-year-old first-year physics student at the university, who was found yesterday on Redcar seafront. According to her flatmate, she failed to come home the other night after studying late at the library."

Dave shook his head as he looked along the length of the board once more. "They're getting younger."

Jenny gulped. "You don't suppose…?" Dave remained silent. "What's he getting out of it, sir?"

"I don't know, Sergeant. I just don't know." He gave a heavy sigh. "Okay, let's go over what we do know. What's his MO?"

Jenny gave a sigh of her own. "Sick, that's what it is. He slashes them repeatedly with some type of kitchen knife, yet they all seem to have put up no resistance. All the women he's then raped after wounding them and then he literally stabs them to death!"

"And these attacks are not only brutal but sloppy and crude," Dave continued for her. "He clearly has no medical knowledge and seems to be something of an amateur."

"Yet he's able to control his victims and leave no detectable trace of himself at any of the crime scenes," Jenny completed, "indicating that he's actually a lot cleverer than he seems. It just doesn't make sense."

Dave shook his head again. "I know, Sergeant. I know."

Chapter 8

He pushed the door open and bellowed, "Illumito." He then walked into the room with his staff raised and closed it behind him. The lamps that he had set up around his small living space flickered into life.

He leant the staff against the wall by the door and walked over to the small fridge he kept in the other corner and removed one of the bottles of beer. He opened it with the bottle opener he left hanging on the wall above the fridge. He could have used magic but he preferred to not stress his will out when he was relaxing. Besides which, he'd also come to quite enjoy the simple pleasure of ripping the small lump of metal off the glass bottle with nothing but another strip of metal and his own brute strength to achieve it.

He pulled out the simple wooden chair he kept in one of the the corners of the room and placed it in front of the large wooden bookshelf. He smiled at himself as he drank the sparkling alcoholic liquid and viewed his prizes.

"Who's the best now?" he asked them smugly. "Who's the best now?"

He smiled and took the knife out of his pocket and twirled it in his hand. Suddenly he stopped, took the blade in his right hand and pricked his left index finger with it. A small droplet of thick red liquid slowly oozed out of the tip.

He didn't know why he did that. Maybe it was to make sure that he was still alive and that he wasn't just dreaming.

He didn't really care.

He smiled as he licked his finger and stood up. The pressure was gone for now; he could relax. He'd made his point.

He muttered an incantation under his breath and summoned the staff to his hand. It was time to go to bed. As he reached the door that led to his bedroom, he smiled again, uttered a word as he waved his staff and the lamps flickered out leaving only the glow of his prizes.

Chapter 9

"Damn it!" Amy screwed up the umpteenth piece of notepaper and threw it onto the overflowing pile in, or perhaps a more accurate description would be, on top of, the bin.

"You know, it would be better for the environment if you used your computer."

Amy looked up at her flatmate with a scowl. "Not now, Donna."

"I'm just saying..."

"And I've told you that it helps me to concentrate and see patterns better if I brainstorm by hand."

"Okay," Donna said calmly as she put her hands up spreading her black, painted fingernails. "Like I said, I'm just saying."

Amy curled her lip up slightly; she liked to consider herself liberal but was finding it difficult to be lectured about the moral obligations of saving the planet from a full-blown purple-haired goth, decked out completely in black with more metal in her face than the average medieval ironmongers!

Donna softened slightly and smiled. "Sorry. I'm sure that this isn't easy but I'm just a bit worried about you, that's all. I mean, you've been working on this thing all day without a break and you've had nothing to eat since breakfast."

Amy sighed and rubbed her hand through her hair. "Sorry, you're right. Thanks for looking out for me but I'm honestly okay. It's just that it's not right."

"You don't need to tell me that, Amy..."

"No, I don't mean the killing. Well, of course that's not right. But what I mean is the profile's not right. There's something wrong, something's missing."

"How do you mean?"

Amy sighed again. "Well, actually there's a couple of things. First of all, why isn't he keeping any trophies?"

Donna looked puzzled. "Trophies?"

"Yeah, all sexually motivated serial killers keep them. Bits of their victims so that they can relive the experience later."

"Like Jack the Ripper took his victims' uteruses?"

Amy was silent for a moment, impressed with her flatmate's knowledge of the world's first serial killer. She wondered if it was more to do with Donna's lifestyle or her degree in history. Since the PhD, Donna had been researching ancient Celtic myths. Amy found herself doubting it was the latter. Not wanting to get distracted dwelling on that train of thought, she just answered Donna's question. "Yeah, exactly. But this guy's taking nothing."

Donna thought for a moment. "Photographs?"

"Sorry?"

"Maybe he's taking photographs or using a video camera?"

Amy shook her head. "Not personal enough."

"Okay, well what's the other problem, the fact that he crossed the gender line?"

Amy whistled through her teeth. "That's certainly unusual but it's not the main problem."

"Then what is?"

"That's just it. I don't know!"

Donna frowned. "Well, it's a bit difficult to come up with a solution if you don't know the problem."

Amy gave her a cold, hard stare. "Tell me something I don't know. It's just simply... I don't know, that there's something wrong with the profile. All the attacks have been in a frenzy, but everything he's done has been controlled. I mean, it's just not possible that one person can do both and yet..."

"What?"

"I'm certain that this is being done by a lone offender. Someone who's in a sort of menial office job. Not good enough to get any higher in his organisation, whatever that may be, and has few friends, if any. In short, a total loner who's almost invisible, but at the same time it just doesn't make sense that someone like that could have the ability to do this sort of thing without any help."

Donna was silent for a moment, wondering what to say to encourage her friend. "Have you found anything else out?"

"Possibly." Amy stood up. "But I need to check something first."

Donna watched Amy walk over to the coat stand they kept by the door and remove the long black coat she used during the cooler months from it. "Where are you going?"

"Out. I need to go and see someone before they leave work."

"What, at this time? It's getting a bit late in the day if you want to catch them and, besides, it looks like it's going to rain any minute now."

"Doesn't matter," Amy said as she grabbed her small umbrella and shoved it inside her coat. "This can't wait. Don't wait up for me, I may be a while." With that, she was gone before Donna could even ask where she was going.

Chapter 10

"So what do you think, Doc? Do I pass?"

Mike looked up from the stack of papers on his desk that made up Tracy's latest status report and curled his lip up slightly in a half smile as he looked up at her. He just couldn't get over the young woman's confidence. When he'd done his PhD, he'd been nervous every time he'd gone to see his supervisor, let alone when he had to deliver a status report, especially one that was two weeks overdue. Not that he'd ever had one even a minute overdue, of course!

A part of him thought that maybe he should give Tracy some stern words on how the world works and what responsibility meant, but another part of him couldn't help but admire her courage, and there was something else. "Well, I am disappointed that this has taken so long to get to me, Tracy." He paused, hoping to add some dramatic tension but Tracy didn't even flinch. "But I must say that it was worth the wait."

Her already wide smile seemed to double in size as she flashed her perfectly straight, bright, white teeth. "I told you it would be."

Mike shook his head slightly and sighed. "Your new mathematical formula certainly does provide some interesting models of quantum structure. However, they do need to be extended somewhat..."

"That'll be in the next report, Doc."

"So this isn't your final report?"

"Nah. I've got some more tricks up my sleeve to show you. How about for now I leave that with you to digest while I work on the rest of it?"

Mike looked his research student up and down; it hadn't escaped his notice that instead of her usual student attire of jeans and plain top she was decked out in a short black dress and high heels, as well as more make-up than he'd ever seen her wear. "Would I be right in saying that you're planning to go out tonight?"

Again, she gave him that bright smile. "Thanks, Doc, I knew you'd understand. You enjoy that report."

"Wait, Tracy, I—"

But she was already heading out the door. "I'll catch you later, Doc. Have a good one."

He considered yelling after her for about half a second, but he had better things to do. Though, as he gathered Tracy's report up and put it to one side, he couldn't help but admire her cunning. Coming to drop her report off last thing at the end of the day so that he wouldn't have the chance to review it with her and then to have the gall to go straight our clubbing was amazing. Still, if he was being honest, he was glad she was gone. It was time, it was ready.

He leaned back in his chair as he set up the computer and smiled to himself. He couldn't believe he'd done it. True, he'd had to stay behind in his office for hours every night for the last week, but it was worth it. Although he could have used his home computer, it had nowhere near the processing power of the ones at the university and if this was going to work, he needed all the calculating capability he could get his hands on.

He checked over the code he'd written one last time and then hit the compile button. He was sure he'd now removed all the bugs and, in no time at all, the program was ready. He moved the mouse slowly and deliberately until the cursor was over the run command and clicked once.

He waited patiently for the program to finish and took the time to reach into his bag and bring out an apple to munch on. God, he hoped this worked. He told himself to stop being so pessimistic. He knew it would work; it was a tried and tested science.

It was just as he was throwing the apple core in the bin by his desk that the program finally finished. He waited patiently and observed the readout on the screen.

That couldn't be right.

He printed the results out and read through them again before scribbling a couple of notes in the margin.

He took out the map of the town he had in his bag and spread it out on the table he used for tutorials. Picking up a pen from his desk, he marked out the main co-ordinates on the map. Finally, he circled the result.

It couldn't be.

He went back to the computer and used the diagnostic tools to step through the program. That all seemed in order. He went back to the code and checked it for what must have been the thousandth time; it was all correct.

He walked back over to the table and stared at the map again.

It couldn't be.

The son of a bitch!

He grabbed the map and printout before running out the door.

Chapter 11

"And that's the problem, Professor Lambert. Do you have any ideas what it could be?"

Verity Lambert looked over at the young woman with a critical eye before whistling through her teeth slightly. It wasn't every day that one of her former undergraduate students dropped by to visit her. Especially at 5pm to ask for help with profiling a deranged serial killer. "I must be honest, Amy, you know this isn't really my field. I mean, I'm a clinical psychologist, not a behavioural profiler."

Amy nodded solemnly. "I realise that, Professor, but—"

"And you're not my student anymore, you know. Verity will be fine."

Amy smiled. "Verity, thank you. I realise that but I just need someone else's opinion. A fresh pair of eyes, you know? I mean, it doesn't make sense, does it? He's taking no trophies, crossed the gender line and is able to subdue and control his victims with ease and confidence yet he shows clear signs of a submissive personality, as well as deranged psychosis from the nature of the killings."

Professor Lambert lent back in her chair slowly and placed her hands on top of her mass of curly black hair, trying hard not to let her frustration show. It was her daughter's birthday and she desperately wanted to get home for the surprise party that her husband had organised. However, she did have a soft spot for Amy; she had been one of her better and more enthusiastic students. She could still remember the sense of pride when the young woman had gotten a place studying her PhD down South at one of the best centres of excellence for psychological research in the country. And she never forgot how Amy had kept in touch for the following three years via email to tell her that she wouldn't have got there without her former tutor's support.

As well as all that, Verity did also have a lot of respect for what Amy was trying to achieve and she did want to help any way that she could. After all, she was as scared as anyone else about who the serial killer was going to hurt next. "I'll admit it all seems very strange."

"It just doesn't add up."

Verity gave a sort of half smile; an idea was forming in her mind. "Is there anything that you are certain of?"

Amy exhaled a deep breath and whistled through her teeth. "Well, yeah, I suppose. That is, I think I've managed to identify some aspects of his personality but—"

Wanting to get home, Verity raised her hand and cut Amy off before she could finish. "Okay, well, if you want my advice, Amy, I think you should be concentrating on that. You need somewhere to start from so try and find out what's important to him and you'll probably find the answers to some of your other questions. Remember, all our behaviour is connected. If you can find the reason that he's concerned with something, anything, you'll find something about him and that..."

"Could lead me to understand the reasons behind his ambiguity." Amy nodded excitedly. "Yeah, that might help. Thanks, Verity."

Professor Lambert smiled warmly. "You're welcome. I hope you don't mind but I have to get home now. Can I give you a lift?"

"Uh, no, I'll be fine, thank you." She got up and shook the professor's hand before leaving.

Chapter 12

Mike was down the stairs, out the door and round the corner to the Order in record time. He pushed on the door twice before he realised he wasn't wearing the talisman and swore under his breath. He pulled it out of his pocket and virtually threw it over himself before ramming the door for a third time; this time it swung open. The spectral butler shimmered down in front of him and barely got out his greeting before Mike marched straight through him. Under normal circumstances, he'd have had trouble remembering the complex route that the treasurer had led him down, but he was in such a mood that he opened his mind and sought out Chris' aura with his psychic power. He found it easily and ran through the hallways like a madman, twisting and turning and nearly falling over three times. He was soon standing outside the vice-mage's office, the large wooden door looming like a shadow in front of him. He actually considered knocking for about half a second but his anger got the better of him and he simply pushed it. He shouldn't have been surprised when it didn't budge an inch but he was undeterred. He slammed his palm against the mass of solid oak and looked within himself and felt his power. He bled it out into his hand and released it into what he knew would be the week spot in the protection ward and the door flew open. The vice-mage was sat behind his desk for about half a second before he shot up; his face seeming to instantaneously take on a colour that Mike had never seen before.

The older man snorted under his breath. "What is the meaning of this, Michael?" His voice was hoarse, deep and clearly full of fury.

Mike stood there, staring at him, and found himself breathing in and out to rhythm. "Who is he?" he demanded.

"What the hell are you talking about?"

Mike held up the collection of papers he had clasped in his hand. "He's here. I worked it out."

"Who's here? Me? Mr Simpkins?" The vice-mage gestured in front of his desk and Mike noticed for the first time that the little treasurer was sitting there nervously. Chris turned to him and said, "Mr Simpkins, would you go and fetch Keeper Rawlins for me, please?"

Simpkins looked up at Mike nervously. Mike suddenly realised how much he must have terrified the poor little man when he burst in. He probably didn't realise that Mike knew Chris' spells so well that he knew exactly the flaw in all his wards; of course, Simpkins may have been more concerned about the fact that Mike hadn't used a staff! Shit, what was he thinking? Simpkins wasn't moving; he was obviously still nervous. Mike decided the best move was to try and smooth things over. He gave the little man a slight smile. "It's all right, Mr Simpkins. I just want to have a chat with Chris."

Simpkins gave a nervous little smile, gripped his staff that was lying by the chair, muttered a word under his breath and disappeared in a puff of smoke. Despite his initial anger subsiding slightly, Mike fixed Chris with a hard stare.

"That was foolish, Michael."

Mike ignored him and snapped his own fingers, causing the door to shut again. "I'm warning you, Chris. Don't play with me; I'm not in the mood."

"What is your problem, Michael?"

It was at that point that the door burst open again and Jon entered, brandishing his staff. The look on his face was that of such shocked, contorted fury that Mike didn't know whether to be afraid or laugh his head off. "What the hell do you think you're doing?" Jon screamed. Mike sniffed uncomfortably.

"Stop waving that thing around, Jonathon," Chris said. Mike was surprised at the vice-mage's defence of him and wasn't sure if Jon would obey but the keeper lowered the staff without taking his eyes off Mike for half a second. Chris then continued, "I would appreciate it if you'd tell us exactly what you're going on about, Michael, and I suggest that you make it quick."

Mike looked over at him and then back over at Jon. "Shut the door." The keeper looked over at Chris. The vice-mage nodded his head slightly. Jon waved his staff and the office door closed. When Mike was satisfied, he started with his explanation. "Have either of you ever heard of geographic profiling?" They were both silent. "Why am I not surprised?" He slammed the map and printout on Chris' desk.

The vice-mage looked down at them. "What is this?"

Mike seemed to ignore him. "Contrary to popular belief, human behaviour isn't complex like people think; it can all be mapped and analysed and all it takes is mathematics."

"What are you drivelling on about?" Jon demanded. "We're not interested in any of your unenlightened rubbish."

"Let him finish, Jonathon," Chris stated in a tone that was both final and emotionless. It was one Mike remembered well from his training days.

"The point I'm making is that it's possible to take human behaviour and turn it into a mathematical formula to work out from things they have done exactly where they've been."

"Now you're making no sense at all," Jon sniped.

Mike scowled at him. "The point I'm making is that it's possible to mathematically calculate the location of a serial killer's home based on the locations of his killings."

Jon almost smirked. "You don't mean…"

"Yeah, I've worked out where Mad Jack lives based on the locations of where all the victims were found." He slammed his finger onto the map over the red circle he'd identified as the epicentre. "And it's here."

The other two men just stood there and stared at him. Suddenly, Jon burst into laughter. "You seriously believe that one of the enlightened is an insane murderer? You arrogant fool."

Mike breathed heavily. "This is no joke, Rawlins. Now, who is it?"

"You think we'd hide someone like that?" Chris asked suddenly.

Mike looked over to him. "Like you told me. You keep the Code."

He barely heard the swish, but he immediately felt the coldness of the metal against his neck. It took him about half a second to realise that Jon had drawn the sword from his cane. "Whatever you are insinuating you will withdraw it and apologise immediately, you unenlightened outsider!"

Mike was silent. For most of his life he'd feared the power of the keepers, but his anger was so great that he found himself standing steady. Well, almost steady! Suddenly, Chris spoke. "I told you to put that away, Jonathon."

"But, sir..."

"Do as I say."

Begrudgingly, the keeper lowered his blade but he kept it out of its sheath; his eyes remaining fixed on Mike the whole time. Chris gave them both his smile that showed no warmth. "Michael, I understand that you're upset about your student's death." He paused; Mike could tell that he was waiting for a response. When he didn't give one, the vice-mage continued. "However, if you think that one of us has been committing these terrible acts and you think that any of your unenlightened theories will make us admit it, you're a fool." Mike didn't need to turn his head to see Jon's smirk. "Now I suggest you leave before you embarrass yourself further."

Mike stared at the old man for a few seconds, then grabbed the map and printout from the desk. "I'm warning you, Chris, I will find out who he is."

"And then you'll apologise for accusing one of us."

Mike said nothing more but made a point of giving Jon a dirty look before slamming the door on his way out.

Chapter 13

Amy pulled her long coat around herself tightly and shivered. She really wished she'd taken the time to put her scarf on before she had left her flat. Not only was it cold but it was totally dark now, oh the joy! It was well past six when she finally left Professor Lambert's office, but for some reason she couldn't bring herself to head home just yet.

Although the north side of the university led to the main student drag and was hence filled with bars, clubs, people and noise, the south side (where she was now) backed on to Southfield Road, where there were only a few offices and shops. Since all of these closed by five, this area was often almost completely quiet during the evenings.

Amy had never really been over this side of the university before, certainly not at this time of the evening and the quiet was somewhat eerie. All she could hear was her own footsteps clomp and click as she walked up and down. It seemed unnatural not to have noise around the university; no students running to class, no screaming, no shouting. Even though this was the quiet side of the university, she still expected the odd partygoer or pub-crawler to pass through but so far, she hadn't seen a soul. She guessed that she shouldn't be surprised; with the sixth victim found just yesterday Mad Jack had probably put all but the hardest drinkers off going out.

God, what the hell was she doing? Here she was out late in the town centre trying to find the reason that her profile wasn't working. None of it made any more sense and she was getting frustrated.

She found herself walking aimlessly around the old university building as if in a dream, but her mind was ticking over every detail in a desperate attempt to make sense of it all. The last victim was a student of the uni – could that be significant? Another shiver ran down her spine; she hated the thought of something like that happening here. The place held so many good memories for her from the time she spent there studying her degree in psychology. The nutty professors, the partying, the sneaking out of her house to meet Kev in his dorm... She chuckled to herself under her breath, then she thought of Mad Jack again and the laughter stopped.

Mentally shaking herself down, she left the university grounds and walked round the corner, looking at the old, whitewashed terraced houses. It was then that she felt a small droplet of moisture fall on her head. Damn, it was starting to rain. She pulled out the small umbrella she'd secreted in the inside pocket of her coat and managed to open it just in time before the heavy downpour started. Guess that was God's way of telling her she should go home; a glance at her watch told her that she'd been there for nearly two hours, which certainly seemed to confirm that assumption! She turned her back to the university building and headed toward the direction of her flat.

At the end of the road, she stopped suddenly. Did she just hear something? She turned around and looked all around her; there was nobody there. Then she felt something on the back of her head and she spun around again quickly and took a step back to find...That there was nothing there either. Just a wall covered in the long dark shadow of the next building. She pricked up her ears but all she could hear was the increasingly loud pitter-patter of the heavy rain.

Suddenly, she realised she was holding her breath. God, she had to get a hold of herself. She breathed a sigh of relief before turning back round to carry on toward the main street.

He released his will and stepped out of the shadows, revealing himself to the night, and watched her walk round the corner. This was too good to be true. He looked down at the single brown hair he had plucked from her head and smirked. He took the balaclava out of his back pocket and pulled it over his face. He then gripped his staff and followed her. It was time for him to take his seventh prize.

Mike barged out of the Order into the pouring rain, full of rage and fury. He just couldn't believe their arrogance. He gripped his hand in a fist and felt his power within it. He'd show them, he'd make them...

Suddenly, he felt the sharp pain in his back and he almost screamed. Despite all these years, he still couldn't prepare himself for its intensity. It was like his back was on fire, like a flame that was burning inwards, trying to burn into his very soul.

He bit his lower lip to stop himself screaming and looked within himself to fight the fire until finally he had the darkness under control. Slowly, the pain subsided; he started to pant heavily and had trouble breathing but at least the worst of it was over. Finally, he caught his breath and he breathed a sigh of relief before counting to 10; he had to calm down.

Just like the others, he walked up behind her but stayed a safe distance away. He removed a piece of card from his pocket. He'd already drawn an intricate symbol onto it in his own blood – a set of interconnected stars that were fenced in by a circle approximately an inch in diameter. He placed the hair into the centre of the circle and held it down with his left thumb. He then raised his staff with his right hand and drew up his power. "Cirato, Kiruno," he whispered. Almost instantly, he felt a not unpleasant warmth spread from his right hand through his body into his left hand and onto the piece of card. The symbol glowed slightly in the darkness and the hair fused itself to the card. He smiled to himself as he aimed the staff and pushed the spell out toward the young woman. He felt it hit her squarely on the back. His smile widened as he started to whisper under his breath, "Stop and come to me. Stop, and come to me."

Amy stopped dead in her tracks. Something was wrong. She suddenly felt another cold chill running down her spine. She didn't like this at all; she felt compelled to turn around to go back and she didn't know why. What was wrong with her? She reached into her coat and wrapped her fingers around the crucifix her mother gave her like she always did when she felt nervous. The small cold bit of metal gave her strength and comfort. She smiled and chuckled to herself. *God, you're being silly girl!* she told herself and continued to walk on.

***

What? What was wrong? She'd stopped like all the others, but why hadn't she turned around and walked back to him? Maybe the spell was wrong; he called up his power once more and repeated the incantation. This time she didn't even stop. How was that possible? Who did she think she was? No unenlightened defied his power! He jammed the card into his coat pocket, exchanged the staff into his left hand and ran toward her before reaching back into his coat pocket.

Mike took another deep breath and leaned forward. He couldn't believe how stupid he'd been getting so angry. Now, to make things even worse, it was raining, and his map and printout were getting saturated. He shoved them into his jacket pocket in frustration and felt another surge of pain causing him to double over again. What was he going to do now? He stood there for a minute looking at the rain-soaked pavement, trying to gather his thoughts and took another deep breath. He was winning the battle now and had his emotions back under control, but he still couldn't concentrate properly. Two things brought the pain on, intense emotions or using too much of his power, and it didn't just hurt, it drained him, made him weak. He tried to get his breathing back to something resembling normal by closing his eyes and slowly inhaling and exhaling. He needed to get back to full strength and he was almost there.

Amy continued to walk as if she'd felt nothing. She really had to get more sleep, she was seeing shadows. Perhaps Donna was right and she was getting too involved in this profile. Maybe she should take a break from it for a while and...

"Who the hell do you think you are, bitch?" His left arm was around her chest before she could even turn around; he was holding something like a length of wood in it. "Nobody defies my power." It was then that she saw the knife in his right hand and screamed as she dropped the umbrella.

Mike's head snapped up so quickly that he almost gave himself whiplash. The noise was incredible; he'd never heard such a scream filled with terror before. It was only as he realised the danger that he became aware that his legs were already moving and that he was running around the corner. He heard more than felt the puddles of water splash under his feet as he reached the end of the street and stopped dead. The sight he saw was unbelievable. The man was wearing a mask of some sort and he looked to be strangling the young woman from behind.

Still not fully recovered from his recent bout of anger, Mike found himself shouting without thinking, "Hey, let her go." The pair suddenly stopped struggling and the man took the opportunity to wrap his right arm around the girl's throat. He then spun them both round, and it was only then that Mike noticed the staff in the man's left hand. "Oh shit."

The man snickered as he pointed the length of wood at Mike. His eyes glazed over until they appeared to be nothing more than completely solid white pearls within the eyeholes of the mask and, in a horse voice, he yelled, "Firara, Firugo." A huge ball of flame erupted from the lump of timber.

Instinctively, Mike dived to the right and landed in the middle of the empty road. The fireball smashed into the pavement where he'd been standing and erupted in an explosion of black and red fire. Without thinking, Mike rolled himself over onto one knee and stared at the man. The girl's eyes had taken on a look of shocked terror. The man was still in a spell-casting trance state and the end of his staff was continuing to smoulder.

Mike looked around. There was no help; his options were limited. He had to do something before that nut blasted him with another fireball. He slammed his hand onto the wet tarmac in front of him, feeling the rough ground dig into his palm as he screamed, "Kraven, I summon you."

A black mass spread out from his hand like a living sea made from syrupy tar, eventually taking on the form of a large black circle that was about six feet in diameter. The man stumbled back in shocked surprise as beams of bright white light suddenly shot out from Mike's hand and overlaid themselves on the circle to form a six-point star. Almost as soon as they stopped, the centre of the star exploded into what seemed to be a massive eruption of black and white fire and something resembling a large bat shot out from the centre of the circle. The creature soared into the air with a high-pitched screech and looped round to zoom toward the man and the terrified girl.

The man virtually threw the girl against the wall with a horrific thud and she slumped to the floor into a still, lifeless, lump. Meanwhile, the masked man ducked down and the large bat-like creature flew over his head. The circle faded and Mike continued to kneel on the floor, feeling water seep into the knees of his jeans as he panted heavily and tried to think what to do. Kraven was a powerful familiar but summoning him in such an open area was risky to say the least. Thank God this part of town was so empty at this time of night.

Noticing the girl's still form, Mike dashed over to her and knelt down beside her. A quick touch of her neck told him that she was still alive but she seemed to have knocked her head pretty badly against the wall. The man in the mask was getting up now and Mike could see Kraven flying back round for another attack. He drew up his power into the palm of his right hand, preparing an attack of his own and stood over the girl. If the nut tried to attack him or her, he was ready to counter and if the lunatic tried to run, Kraven would get him. Either way, there was no way that this guy could get away now.

But instead of launching himself at either of them, the man stood his ground and looked back and forth between them frantically. Suddenly, he spun his staff around and slammed it onto the pavement with a scream of, "Hiraz!" Immediately, a massive flash of intense, bright light exploded around the man. Mike just managed to cover his eyes with his arms. He heard Kraven scream then a strange, confused thumping sound. The next thing Mike knew, he was being knocked up against the wall. He looked up and the man was gone. Looking down, he found Kraven was lying on top of him with his large leathery wings covering his face.

"Are you okay, mate?" Mike asked anxiously.

"I can't see," the familiar replied in a raspy voice.

"The light's gone. Try now."

Kraven moved his wings down slowly and blinked his pitch-black eyes nervously. His pointy ears twitched and the black bandanna he wore round his face wriggled with heavy breathing. "He took me by surprise. Forgive me, Michael, I dishonour you."

Mike smiled as he stood up. It was then that he realised that his right hand felt sore; he looked down to see that it was cut, scraped and had gravel stuck in it. Damn, that was going to be sore in the morning. He rubbed as much of the gravel off as possible and looked at Kraven. "It's okay, mate, we saved the girl. That's the main thing."

Kraven propped himself up and nodded. "True but what should we do now?"

Suddenly Mike's heart started to beat rapidly again. What would they do now? That fight would have certainly got somebody's attention and sooner or later authorities would be around to deal with the fire at the very least. He couldn't leave the girl here, she'd seen too much and, besides, what if that nut came back? What was she doing here anyway? God, there was no time for that now. What could he do? He looked at Kraven. "Can you fly us both back to my office if I cast a veil round you to conceal us?"

Kraven stood up, bowed and nodded. "Of course, my friend. It would be an honour. But do you have enough power?"

Mike nodded. "Yeah, I think so."

He knelt down and gently picked the girl up in his arms. It was then that he finally got a good look at her. He was amazed at how small she was; she couldn't have been taller than five feet and she was so light that even his own chubby, unexercised arms had no trouble lifting her diminutive frame. Even through the pouring rain, he couldn't avoid catching the smell of her delicate perfume blowing in the night air; it smelled sweet like summer flowers and honey. God, he'd always found the scent of women's perfume so intoxicating. She looked to be in her early twenties, with long, curly brown hair and an exquisitely pretty face. Mike found that he had to compose himself to keep his concentration. He was sure he'd seen her somewhere before but he couldn't think about that now.

"Is this hers?"

Mike looked up to see that Kraven was holding a small black umbrella. "Um, yeah, probably. Do you see anything else, like a purse or something? We don't want to leave anything behind that could draw attention to her or us."

"Not that I can see, my friend."

"Cool. Well give me that here and then let's get going."

Kraven laid the collapsed umbrella on top of the young woman's chest, then flapped his wings and took to the sky. Mike closed his eyes and concentrated. He felt Kraven grab his shoulders with his hand-like clawed feet and lift them into the air. Mike hoped that the girl didn't wake up as he wriggled his fingers underneath her to cast the spell. He pulled the darkness around them into a veil; hoping that it would be enough to keep them protected from prying eyes. He kept his own eyes firmly shut as they jerked through the night air, trying to ignore the unnatural sensation that came from having no solid ground beneath his feet.

The journey didn't take long as they were still not far from the university and Mike soon felt the satisfaction of the stone pavement underneath him once more. He opened his eyes and released the spell to find they were standing next to the entrance of the university car park. Kraven flapped down beside them and retracted his wings so that they once more took on the appearance of more arm-like limbs.

The university car park was a two-storey square building with a single, large entrance for both cars and people. The university had hoped that a single barrier on the incoming road would prevent unauthorised use but Mike knew all too well that the downside was that it didn't keep out drunks and other trespassers during the day, let alone the night. Staff were therefore advised to only leave their cars in after dark at their own peril.

The lights in the car park had long gone out and the entrance now looked like the forbidding mouth of a pitch-black cave. Mike shivered as he nodded toward it and Kraven followed him inside while keeping a watchful eye out for any trouble. Mike's footsteps echoed around the empty building as he cautiously carried the girl into the large structure.

Fortunately, Kraven's bare feet ensured he made no noise. Mike was amazed that his eyes adjusted to the dark fairly quickly and he soon found his car and thankfully nothing, or more importantly, nobody, else.

"I see you still have the same vehicle," Kraven said politely as they approached the small Ford Focus.

Mike nodded as he handed the girl to the familiar. "Yeah and I see you still have the same swords," he replied, indicating the two samurai swords strapped across Kraven's back like a large 'X'. Kraven said nothing but Mike could tell he was smiling under his mask.

He unlocked the car and they strapped the girl into the passenger seat. "Where will you take her?" Kraven asked, concerned.

"Back to my home."

"Then what?"

Mike shrugged. "I'll figure something out. You'd better get going in case anyone comes in and sees you. Thanks for your help again, mate. You were great, as always."

Kraven bowed. "Always an honour, my friend." He released the tension, shimmered into black smoke and vanished.

Mike quickly got into his car and drove off.

Chapter 14

He stood as still as a post, not moving, not even breathing. Silently, he watched them take to the sky and vanish. Only then did he release the spell and step out of the shadows. He drew a single breath of the cold night air into his lungs and snarled. Damn that sorcerer! How dare he take his prize? He shook his staff violently in the air. Nobody defied his power, he'd make him suffer. He snarled again and started to breathe in and out heavily.

Suddenly, something else crept into his senses along with the cold night air. Something that smelt musty and smokey like cheap cigars. Wait a minute, smokey? He looked over at the pavement; the Spirt Flame that he had summoned was still burning and glowing brightly. That meant trouble; it was bound to attract attention and that meant that the unenlightened's law keepers could be there any second or, even worse, the keepers or maybe even the knights! He had to get away and quickly.

He looked around frantically but there was no side alley or back street to duck into. It was no good; he had to use his power, but he'd never tried to use a veil while moving. His breath quickened; he had no choice. He gripped his staff firmly in both hands and murmured under his breath. His power pulled the shadow back round him and he ran up the street to the corner. He knew it was dangerous moving while veiled. It was extremely difficult to keep an effective one up while mobile but he had no choice. He reached the corner and darted round without even thinking about where he was going; he just kept running.

When he reached the main street, he released his power and the veil faded from around him. He was now out of breath from having run all the way and was panting heavily. He steadied himself on his staff as he tried to catch his breath. Damn that sorcerer! This was all his fault. When he finally felt like he was breathing normally, he looked up and surveyed his surroundings. It was only then that he realised that he was on one of the main roads and that there was some commotion on the opposite corner.

He quickly ducked into the doorway of a nearby shop and peered round to see where the noise was coming from. It appeared to be generated from a bar at the end of the road. It was one of those new 'trendy' places that played loud music. He hated places like it. All those young people doing whatever they liked, consuming all that vile fluid. They thought they owned the world. They knew nothing. They were the worst of the unenlightened as far as he was concerned; he hated them all. Damn it, the pressure was unbearable now. What could he do? He needed release. He had to get back; maybe seeing his prizes would help.

He was just turning around when suddenly he heard another sort of noise coming from the bar. He turned back and saw that the doors had burst open and two figures were staggering out. They were both showing so much flesh that it was obscene. The blonde one on the left was leaning on the brunette.

He paused for a moment, then, saying a quick incantation under his breath, he reached into the staff with his will and drew some of its power into himself. He pulled the power down his arm and up through his body into his head and then looked up.

"Are you sure you'll be okay getting home, Tracy?" He could hear the brunette's words clearly now.

"Oh, I'll be fine thanks, Nat. My dorm's just round the corner."

"Well, as long as you're sure. I mean, you know with that nut wandering around…"

"Oh, for God's sake, I've told you don't worry about him, girl. If he crosses my path, I'll give him what for. You just get yourself home."

"Okay, as long as you're sure but just promise me you'll be careful and go straight home."

"Yes, Mum, I promise."

With that, the brunette flagged down a passing taxi, got in and was driven away. The blonde girl waved after her for a few seconds then walked down the road toward him. He leaned against the doorway, quietly uttered a few words and drew the shadow round himself again. This was too good to be true. The fates were clearly smiling on him tonight. A prize that deserved to be taught a lesson in respect.

He waited as still as a statue as she approached his hiding place, then, as she walked past, he reached out and plucked a single strand of her blonde hair from the back of her head. She was so inebriated that she didn't even flinch. He released the shadows once more and dug another piece of card with blood symbols drawn onto it from his inside pocket. After placing the single blonde strand onto the card, he repeated the incantation he'd used earlier. "Cirato, Kiruno." Once more, he felt the power flow from the staff into himself and onto the card, fusing the hair to it. Once more, he forced the spell out of the staff toward her. Damn, his power was dwindling. He needed to get back and recharge, but he felt the spell hit her and he just couldn't miss this opportunity now. Especially since he had her name! He concentrated hard and whispered, "Stop, Tracy. Stop."

The girl stopped.

"Come to me, Tracy."

She turned round and walked back toward him. He stepped out of the doorway and she stopped in front of him. "Uh, who are—"

"Shh, Tracy," he said as he raised his hand, "don't speak." She fell silent. "Step closer." She did as he said and he put his arm round her. "Come with me." With that, he murmured another incantation to pull the shadow veil around them both and walked her away.

Chapter 15

The last thing Amy remembered was being thrown through the air.

This was the end. She knew it.

What the hell had happened? God, what had she got herself into?

That guy with the knife. His staff was on fire. No, it created fire!

And the other man and that creature! What was it?

God, what did it matter now? Why hadn't she listened to Dave?

Dave. Suddenly all she could think of now was how horrible she'd been to her brother the last time she'd ever seen him.

She couldn't see or hear anything now.

She wondered if this was Heaven or Hell, or maybe it was something else.

Then, she felt something. It was wet, it was cold and it was on her face. What was going on?

"Are you okay?"

A voice. Was it the voice of God? No, wait, she recognised it. It was then that she realised that she could breathe. She wasn't dead!

Slowly she opened her eyes. The light was bright and she had to blink twice before her vision adjusted to it. For another brief moment, she thought maybe she was dead and that the old cliché about a light at the end of a tunnel was true, but the effect was spoilt when she realised that someone was tapping a cold wet towel on her forehead.

When her eyes finally adjusted to the light, she found that it was a man with a round face and receding hairline. Despite everything that had happened to her, she couldn't help thinking that he looked like a nightclub bouncer. It took her about three seconds before she recognised him and sat up sharply.

"You." As soon as she said it, she started to feel light-headed and worried that she might pass out again.

"Easy," the man said as he steadied her and helped her to sit up straight. His touch was warm and gentle but clumsy, like he was nervous. "You took a nasty knock to the head. You shouldn't move too much."

"You're that guy with the creature," She managed after she'd recomposed herself.

He smiled at her nervously. "I don't suppose there's any chance that I can convince you that all that was just a dream, can I?" She frowned at him. "No, I guess not."

Now feeling a bit better, she carefully readjusted herself to a more comfortable seating position and realised she'd been lying on a very soft and comfortable two-seater sofa in a warm, ordinary-looking lounge. A gas fire was glowing brightly on the back wall, giving out a comforting, warm flame. Her coat and umbrella had been laid out with care on the wood panel flooring in front of it to dry out. She was also surprised to find that the walls were not pitch black but a bright cream colour and a set of energy-saving light bulbs illuminated the room from a fancy light fitting in the ceiling above. She turned back to the man. "Who are you and where am I?"

"Uh, Michael, Michael Walker." He stretched his hand out hopefully but she didn't shake it. He dropped it down. "Sorry, you're in my home, in Redcar. Don't worry, you're safe here."

Suddenly, an important thought entered her head. "What happened to that other guy? The one with the knife." She paused briefly as realisation suddenly hit her. "Wait, that must have been Mad... Oh my God!"

"Please, it's okay. He can't get you here."

"What happened to him?"

Michael Walker paused for a moment and looked almost sheepish. "I'm sorry. I tried to stop him, I swear I tried, but..." He sighed. "He got away, I'm so sorry."

"That creature of yours couldn't stop him?"

"It's not that simple. I'm sorry but he blinded us with some sort of flash of light and..." He sighed. "He somehow vanished."

Amy paused for a moment and looked into his pale blue eyes. Her mother had always told her that the eyes were the gateway to the soul, that they were the truest part of someone, and the only part of a person that could never lie. As she looked into his now, she found herself saying, "I believe you." As she said it, she watched something like a smile creep across his face. She was about to smile herself when she realised something else. "Wait a minute; how the hell did I get here?"

"Oh, there was nothing magical about that, I drove you here, uh, from my office. It was just round the corner. You see, I work at the university and..."

"Hold on a minute. Did you say magical?"

He tried to smile awkwardly. "Well, uh, that is, I mean, uh, hey, don't I know you from somewhere?"

"Don't change the subject."

"You were at the police station; you ran into me. What were you doing there?" Amy was silent. "Are you a police officer?" She was still silent. "Don't worry; I'm not going to harm you or anything. In fact, you're free to go whenever you like but I just wanted to try and explain…"

"Then start giving me some answers. What the hell's going on here? Who the hell was that crazy guy with the knife? More importantly, what was he? In fact, more to the point, what are you?"

Michael Walker was silent for a moment. When he finally spoke, his voice was barely more than a whisper. "Do you really want to know?"

Chapter 16

Mike knew it was a cliché, but he honestly could remember his first day at the Academy of Magic like it was yesterday. That moment when he stepped off the train was such a mixture of excitement and fear that he kept having to catch his breath. He'd only been the apprentice of Christopher Saban for a year when he was accepted, but his master was eager for him to start his studies as soon as possible.

It was a terrifying thought at first, having to go so far away from home at such a young age, but as soon as Master Saban told him of what he would learn there, he knew he had to go. His mother wasn't too thrilled with the idea but his father managed to convince her that it was the best thing for him. So, after a lot of persuasion and with a great deal of reluctance, she finally gave him permission to attend the Academy for a few months each year, but this didn't stop either of them getting emotional as he got on the train at Darlington.

As it pulled into Cardiff station, Master Saban told him this was their stop and to collect his things. Mike remembered having to drag the small suitcase his mother had packed for him, as well as carry the new backpack that had the staff his father had given him stuffed inside along with his mother's gift of a new pad of notepaper and associated pens and pencils. "Do we have far to go from the station, sir?"

"I told you there'll be a minibus waiting to collect us when we get outside. It's not too long from there."

Mike had never heard of a minibus before and wondered what it was as he struggled onto the platform. He wondered if it was anything like the big red ones that he saw on television that were supposed to be down in London. Maybe it was a miniaturised bus, maybe everyone got in and it would shrink so that they could get into a secret tunnel to take them to the Academy of Magic. He couldn't wait.

He found it really difficult to contain his disappointment when he discovered that a minibus was nothing more than a glorified van with seats in it. Especially when said seats were even more uncomfortable than the ones on the train he'd just rode on. To make matters worse, it was rocking from side to side and rattling like a baby's toy. He remembered how he and Master Saban were the only passengers as he looked out the window and watched Cardiff city centre melt away into the Welsh countryside. He started to wonder if he'd made a big mistake; if this was the best that the Academy of Magic could do, what was he going to learn? When he'd first read his father's Grimoires, magic seemed so amazing, so exciting; now he wondered if it was true what the unenlightened said and there really was no such thing, just tricks and sleight of hand.

"We're almost there," Master Saban told him as the minibus pulled into the entrance way of what looked like a park. A sign that bore the legend, 'Wildlife Protected Area. Keep Out' was erected next to a pair of huge, ugly-looking iron gates. Their driver placed his hand onto a strange symbol that was etched onto the dashboard and closed his eyes briefly. Mike watched as the symbol glowed ever so slightly under the man's palm and the large iron gates slowly creaked open to allow them entry. "Was that more to your liking?" Master Saban asked him.

Mike had to admit that he was impressed with the driver's little display of magic but even more so with Master Saban's insight into what he'd been thinking. It was the first time that he'd seen the old man smile, but for some reason he found he didn't like it. The smile seemed wrong to him somehow, like there was something missing from it. Still, he thought he'd better reply to his master's question. "Uh, it was pretty cool, Master," he replied nervously.

"Wait until you see this." Master Saban's words were the same emotionless monotone as always, which made it impossible for Mike to tell the older man's mood, so he really had no idea what to expect.

As they drove through the gates, Mike peered up front between the seats to watch their journey through the vehicle's windscreen as they passed through a seemingly endless road lined with trees. Then suddenly, as the vehicle passed between a particular pair of large royal oaks whose branches seemed to join together and make an archway, the vision through the windscreen started to contort and shimmer almost as if they were passing through a sort of misty fog. That wasn't all though, Mike wasn't just seeing something; he was feeling it too. His body felt heavy, like something vast was weighing down upon him, something intangible and powerful. Then, as he slowly started to see a large, shiny white shape materialise in the distance, he felt the weight start to lift off of him and almost immediately he knew what was happening.

"A veil!" he cried excitedly. "We're passing through a veil."

"Very good, my young apprentice," Master Saban said with the same emotionless voice and the same empty smile. "And that," he said, pointing out the windscreen, "is the Academy of Magic."

Mike watched in awe and fascination as the huge, grand structure materialised in front of them. It was magnificent, like a gigantic mansion made out of solid white marble. Its smooth, shiny surface reflected the sun so brightly that he had to use his hand to shield his eyes, but he couldn't look away. He was just too excited.

As they walked through the doors of the magnificent ancient building, Mike knew he'd made the right choice. His first sight as he walked through the entrance hall, dragging his suitcase behind him with one hand and his backpack on his other shoulder, was something that someone of his age could only describe as incredible. The grand entrance hall was packed with people. Some were rushing up and down, running errands, while others were sat at desks covered in papers where people were queueing to fill out forms or ask questions.

"Wait here while I register you," Master Saban told him sternly.

"Yes, Master, of course."

"Don't move from this spot."

Mike stood still and watched his master join one of the queues of people. He looked around at all the excitement with fascinated eyes. Suddenly, he was drawn to an old man who, like everyone else in the Academy, was wearing long flowing robes. His were of a shiny silvery colour that set off his snow-white beard and shiny bald head. The man was twirling a staff in his arms and muttering under his breath. Mike waited with eager anticipation as he watched the old man strike the floor with his staff and a symbol Mike had never seen before formed itself out of the beams of shiny white light that shot out from the base of the staff. At the centre where all the beams of light crossed, an eruption occurred and out popped a strange creature that climbed up the wizard's side and perched itself upon his shoulder.

Mike couldn't help but stare at the strange creature; it was like nothing he'd ever seen before. It resembled some sort of monkey, about two feet in height, with long, scrawny limbs and light brown fur. But Mike had never seen a monkey with sharp, pointy black wings sticking out of its back before! That wasn't the only thing about it though, the creature's eyes looked wrong; they were too wise, too knowing, too human.

Then, as Mike looked at the creature, it smiled broadly like a Cheshire cat. Mike was shocked but tried to be polite and smile back. He could have sworn that both the creature and the old man laughed but it didn't bother Mike at all. To him, it was incredible; he'd read about such powers but had never seen anything like it. For the first time in his life, he felt like he belonged. No more sneaking around to practise spells; here they were performed openly.

"That was a familiar." Mike looked up to see Master Saban returning toward him.

"Yeah, I know, I've read about them," Mike said excitedly. "Will I learn how to summon them here?"

"Perhaps," his master replied, "if you work hard enough."

It was then that Mike promised himself that he would dedicate himself to his studies with all his energies, so that he could become a great wizard like his master. He wouldn't let him down.

He spent five years going to the Academy, learning as much about the Arts as he could. He made many friends, and a few enemies. Even when he finished his studies and was welcomed into the Order of The Cunning Ones, he stayed at the Academy and continued to seek more great truths.

Until that one fateful day when his entire world changed once again.

Chapter 17

Amy sat on the edge of the settee and stared at Michael Walker. "So let me get this straight. You're a wizard who went to Hogwarts magic school and you belong to some secret cult of wizards?"

Mike frowned and shook his head. "Okay, a few things. Firstly, the Academy of Magic isn't Hogwarts; it's a sort of British university of magic."

"Then why were you there so young?" She interrupted him without thinking, causing him to make another face.

"It's not like that. Anyone who knows about magic can go there to learn more about the Arts; there are students there from something like eight to 80 years old." He ignored the sceptical look on her face and carried on. "Secondly, the Order of the Cunning Ones isn't a cult; it's part of the Anglican Church!"

Now she was shocked. "Say what?"

"And finally," he said, carrying on like she said nothing, "I'm no longer a wizard. I left the Order."

Amy stiffened. "Why?" she asked suspiciously.

He paused for a moment before replying, "I realised that not all the truth of the world was found in the teachings of magic. So I left to study science."

"Say what? Now you're expecting me to believe you're a scientist as well?"

"Theoretical physicist." She stared at him with sceptical eyes. His own took on a look of slight surprise and when he spoke again, his voice took on a tone of somewhat mild amusement. "You can believe that I'm a former wizard who summoned a familiar in front of you tonight but you can't believe I could also be a scientist?"

"It is a little hard to swallow."

He laughed nervously. "I suppose it is, but I swear it's the truth. Here, look, I'll prove it." He reached into one of his pockets and took out a small card which he handed to her.

She nervously took it and found that it had Teesside University's emblem in one corner along with text that read:

Dr Michael Walker, Bsc, PhD, MIoP
Quantum Physics Researcher
Physics Research Department
School of Science & Technology

Along with this was a series of contact information.

"You can keep that if you like," he said with a nervous smile. "Look I don't want to lie to you but at the same time you've got to appreciate that I could be risking my life telling you all this..."

"Yeah, I already guessed that part," she said as she popped the card into her pocket, taking the opportunity to check that her purse and keys were still accounted for. "What I want to know is how all this is kept secret."

"There's a Code."

"A Code?"

Mike took a deep breath. "It's not so much a law as a philosophy. It basically amounts to 'Don't ask. Don't tell.' At least, unless you're sure. Basically, you don't tell the unenlightened…"

"The unenlightened?"

"People who have no knowledge about the Arts." He could see she wasn't impressed, but he pressed on. "Basically, if you want to tell someone who's not aware of magic, it's on your own head."

"Who enforces it?"

"The Orders. They believe they're protecting their own from the masses with torches and pitchforks, I suppose."

"How do the Orders enforce it?"

He looked down awkwardly. "I'd rather not say."

She started to feel uneasy. "So why have you told me?"

Mike stiffened again. "I'm not really sure. I guess I thought with you being a police officer I could trust you."

"I'm not a copper." He looked shocked. Amy was surprised herself that she'd told him so openly.

"Then what are you?

"I'm a criminal profiler and the police have asked me to produce a—" She stopped abruptly.

"What?" he asked.

"My God, that's it."

"Sorry?"

"That's what's missing!" Mike gave her a confused look and she realised she was letting her mind wander. "Sorry, please could you sit down. I want to tell you something."

Mike was about to sit on the settee beside her when he realised something. "Okay, but do I at least get your name?"

Amy gave him a long, hard stare. Could she trust him, should she trust him? Finally, she replied, "Amy. Dr Amy Walsh." This time she offered him her hand and he shook it gently with a smile.

He had his guard up and didn't get a strong shock from her emotions, but he did find the touch of her hand electrifying!

Mike listened to her story intently but found it very difficult to keep his concentration. Sitting so close to her made him feel nervous. He'd always been shy and reserved, particularly around beautiful women and he was sat so close to her that all he could smell was her marvellous perfume. That wonderful scent of wild flowers and sweet honey was just so damn distracting. Finally, she completed her explanation.

"So you're putting together one of those behavioural profiles so that the police can find that maniac who killed Kerry?" he finally asked her.

Mike watched as she looked up sharply and her eyes widened. "Kerry? As in Kerry Jones, the last victim?"

Mike closed his eyes. "Yeah, she was one of my students."

"One of your students?"

"That's why I was at the police station. I was identifying her. I was her personal tutor."

"Oh my God, of course, she was a physics student at the university. I'm so sorry. I mean, I didn't realise."

He opened his eyes and looked at her again. "That's okay." He found himself smiling slightly; the fact that she had warmed to him enough that she felt his pain hadn't missed Mike's attention and he tried to hide the tiny sense of pleasure that came over him.

"So was that how you found him?"

"Uh, well, that is actually... Hey, wait a minute, what do you mean how I found him?" Mike bit his lip; she probably still didn't trust him completely.

Could he trust her?

He had no choice; he'd told her too much already.

He reached over to his jacket that he'd laid on the chair's arm and pulled out the rain-soaked crumpled papers he'd shoved inside the pocket as he'd left the Order. He laid the map out on his coffee table and she looked at it with a puzzled expression. "What's this?" she asked, intrigued.

"A geographic profile." She looked up sharply. "Based on where he's committed his crimes, I've used a mathematical formula to calculate the most likely area that he originates from."

Amy's eyes lit up. "Yeah, I've heard of it. You mean you came up with this?"

Mike bit his lip shyly then gave her a proud smile. "Yeah, I wanted to find the guy so nobody else would die. I thought at first that I could maybe use magic to find him, but when I realised that was impossible, someone made me realise that I could use science, or even just maths."

Amy stared at the map. She looked genuinely impressed. "So this is how you found him? This is excellent, I mean it pinpoints down his location to a much smaller area than my profile ever could." She circled her finger around the mark Mike had made then tapped it, before saying, "But I still don't know why he's staying around here."

Mike wriggled slightly in his seat. "Yeah, I don't either," he lied.

"So why's he doing this?"

Mike looked up at her again sharply. "What?"

"Why's he doing this? Is this all part of some weird magical ritual or something? Like, if he kills 13 people, he gets supreme power or something like that?"

"Uh, no, I mean, I don't think so. I mean, I didn't even know the nut was a wizard until tonight, I just wanted to find the guy..."

"Okay, it's all right, it doesn't matter. We'll work it out."

Mike looked up at her, surprised. "Sorry?"

"Well, don't you see? This is what was missing from my profile. I didn't know that the killer could do magic, or how he could use it to control his victims. Now you can teach me."

Mike stiffened again. "Woah, wait a minute. You want me to teach you magic?"

She shook her head and waved her hand. "No, no, I'm not asking you to teach me your secrets. But can't you show me some of the principles, or at least some more of what you can do? From that I could extrapolate his personality and pinpoint down who he is. You can then take that to the Order and they can hand him over to the authorities. What do you say? I mean you did say you wanted to find this guy, right?"

"Woah, look, hold your horses a minute. I mean there's very little chance that the Order will listen to you or me. Like I said, I'm no longer a part of that world."

"But you know about it. And that's what I need to know. And if the Order won't do anything, well then, we'll have to find him and take him to the police."

"Wait, calm down a minute..."

"Do you want to avenge your student or not?"

Mike sat there for a long time. He did want to find him and he did want to stop him. But it wasn't his job to stop him. Then again, Jon and Chris weren't going to do anything. He should really contact the knights. "Look, I'd like to help but…"

"Please." She reached out and grabbed his hand. "I won't tell anyone you helped me. You said the magical community doesn't want its existence known, right? So we find out who Mad Jack is, and you take his staff; you said that was the source of his power, right?"

"Yeah, but…"

"Then we can call the police to arrest him so he can face justice."

"You make it sound like it's simple."

"It is simple."

"Did anyone ever tell you how crazy you can be?"

"Yeah, most of my family, and my ex-boyfriend. Look, do we have a deal or not?"

Mike was planning to say no, but after hearing that last statement he found himself saying, "Yeah, okay. You've got a deal."

Chapter 18

'Damn it!'

He was really starting to get frustrated now. He stepped away from the table into the corner of the room so that he could take a breather. He gave a long exhale and wiped the sweat off his forehead with the back of his arm, transferring some of the sticky red fluid onto his face in the process, before swearing under his breath.

This one was more difficult than the others. He'd used up all the power in his staff fighting that damn sorcerer. He needed to recharge it as soon as possible. That meant he had to get back to the Order, and quickly, but he couldn't think of doing that now. He had to finish what he started, even though he was exhausted.

Strapping her down to the table had been a nightmare; she'd kicked and screamed like crazy and it had taken all of his strength to get the job done. Still, he'd finally managed to get her under control, but he never realised how loud they screamed. He'd had to shove one of his good handkerchiefs into her mouth to keep the bitch quiet.

The pressure was starting to become unbearable now; he had to relieve it soon. He picked up the knife and approached the table once again.

All too soon, the screaming stopped completely and the pressure was gone.

***

Mike tried to keep his head looking straight ahead, locked in the brace position, as he drove Amy Walsh back to her home. He'd managed to wash the gravel out of his hand before leaving his house, but the cuts and scrapes were now getting sore and it hurt somewhat to grip the steering wheel, but that wasn't the only reason he was struggling to concentrate. He didn't need to use his psychic power to tell him that Dr Walsh didn't entirely trust him; and if he was being honest, he wouldn't trust him if he was her! He knew all too well how dangerous and frightening the Arts could be if you knew about them. To see them used without warning and having your life threatened at the same time would probably be enough to send most people over the edge. He suddenly realised how incredibly brave Amy Walsh must be.

He'd driven out of Redcar and back into Middlesbrough town centre, following the directions that she'd given him, and was now heading toward what used to be Aryesome Park. What had once been Middlesbrough Football Club's stadium had, in recent years, been torn down to make way for trendy new flats. Two words that were very uncommon regarding Middlesbrough accommodation, in Mike's opinion, especially those found in the town centre. He'd never really been to this part of town before and as he pulled into the estate, he was surprised to find that the flats were a fairly simple affair. He was expecting a young hotshot criminal profiler to have a bigger place than this. Guess the private sector of the legal profession wasn't as well paid as he thought it was.

"My flat's just round this corner," Amy said as they reached the first junction in the estate. "It's those down at the bottom... Oh no!"

For the first time since they'd left his house, Mike turned round to look at her. "What's wrong?"

She turned toward him and gave a nervous smile. "Oh, nothing. Sorry. This is fine. I'll see you tomorrow at half five, okay?"

"Uh, okay." With that, she got out and dashed toward the flats without looking back.

Mike waved as she entered the main door, but she still didn't turn around or acknowledge him. He gave a heavy sigh and wondered what the hell he'd gotten himself into as he drove off back home.

Amy peered through the small, reinforced glass window in the door and breathed a sigh of relief as she watched Michael Walker drive away. That was a close one. She'd noticed the two cars that were double parked outside as they drove up and she just hoped they weren't all looking out the window. What the hell were they doing here anyway? She took a quick look at her reflection in the glass; thankfully she'd knocked the top of her head so the bump was pretty much camouflaged by her hair so hopefully that would mean that they wouldn't notice it. She made her way up the stairs to the second floor and unlocked her flat door. There were four people standing in the lounge, two men and two women, and they all turned to face her as she walked in.

Her sister was the first to speak, or rather shout, "Where the hell have you been?"

Amy had all the best laid plans of keeping her cool but, like all of her 'discussions' with members of her family, she failed miserably and just ended up stating the word, "Out." She hoped that her tone was deliberate and final, but probably sounded more like the whining of an immature brat.

"Out where?" was her brother's reply, in a voice filled with frustration.

She frowned at him. "You know, I'm getting sick of this. I'm not a kid anymore. What I get up to in my own time is none of your bleeding business."

"It is when you've gone out in the middle of the night without taking your phone and not telling anyone where you've gone!" Emma virtually screamed at her.

Shit, she'd forgotten her phone when she left. She tried to think up some excuse then suddenly realised something else. "Hang on a minute. Exactly what are you two and Kev doing here anyway?"

Her ex-boyfriend looked up and smiled nervously. "Well, I came round to see you and Donna told me you were missing…"

"In other words, you came here to try and find out what I know about 'You-Know-Who' but when you found I was out, you tried to pump Donna for information…"

"Actually," Dave interjected, "he came round and tried to pump Emma and me for information when he found out you weren't here."

"And the reason we're here," Emma said, "is because somebody called me because they were worried about you!"

Amy stared at her siblings for a moment, open-mouthed, then snapped her head over to look at Donna. Her flatmate smiled nervously. "I'm sorry, Amy, but I was worried. I mean, you ran out like that, then you didn't come home and with everything that's been happening..."

"So you called Emma?"

Her flatmate looked sheepish. "I didn't know what else to do."

"So where have you been?" All eyes turned toward Kev.

"Why the hell are you still here, Kev?" Amy snapped suddenly. "Do us all a favour and get out of our flat."

"Oh, come on, Amy. I'm just worried about you, that's all... Hey!" Kev didn't notice Dave grab his arm.

"You heard my sister, Kevin. She doesn't want you around so why don't you just leave?"

"Hey, this is police brutality."

"I'm not on duty."

"And, as a barrister," Emma chipped in, "I'd advise you that, in my opinion, you're trespassing on private property."

"Why don't you take a hint, Kev?" Donna suddenly piped in. "Nobody wants you around, just get out."

Kev looked like he was going to say something, but one look from Amy made him think better of it. Dave released his grip and Kev simply walked between him and Amy without making eye contact with anyone there before dashing out through the door.

"Now, where the hell were you?" Emma yelled again.

Amy drew a long breath and tried hard to keep calm. "If you must know, I went to see my old university lecturer for some advice on helping produce the profile for you."

Dave sneered. "Oh really? Well, you were a bloody long time doing it."

"These things take time!" She suddenly realised that not only was she shouting but that she was standing aggressively with her hands on her hips. She sighed and shook her head. "Look, I'm sorry I made you all worry, but I'm home now and I'm clearly okay, so how about you guys just leave so we can all get to bed?"

Emma and Dave stared at her for a moment and they looked like they was seriously considering another argument, but in the end, both decided to just give up. Emma nodded politely at Donna and headed for the door without another word. Dave followed behind her and just as he reached the door, he turned back to Amy. "Just do us a favour and don't go out late at night on your own until we catch this guy."

"Come on, Dave," Emma yelled from the hallway, "I need to get home. I'm in court tomorrow."

Amy said nothing, but he'd made his point and she nodded as Dave hurried out after Emma. After they'd left and she'd locked the door, Amy turned to Donna, who said, "Look, Amy, I—"

Amy raised her hand. "Please, Donna, don't. Not now. I've had a really long day and an even longer night."

With that, she went to her room and closed the door behind her. She leaned against it and started to wonder what the extent of Michael Walker's powers might be. Maybe, if she was lucky, he could make a couple of people disappear for her!

He wiped the knife down with a cloth before rubbing the sweat off his brow with the back of his right hand. He hung up the heavily stained apron on the nail he'd hammered into the wall and placed the gloves on the nearby bench. There was no doubt about it; that had been the most exhausting one he'd done yet, but it didn't matter. At least the pressure was gone now.

He really needed to get rid of the mess but there was plenty of time to do that later. First he would take his prize back and place it with the others. He smiled to himself as he picked up the jar and left.

Chapter 19

"Don't you agree, Mike? MIKE?"

"Wha...?" Mike suddenly realised that everyone round the table was looking at him and that the head of physics research had just asked him a question. He decided to go for the safe option. "Oh, sorry, Stuart. Yes, absolutely."

Professor Stuart Cooke looked over the horn-rimmed glasses that had slipped down his nose for a moment. His old PhD supervisor had a strong face with gingery designer stubble. His hair loss was the only indication of his advancing age. He was also well-built and still walked tall; Mike always thought that this was a result of his former military service. This didn't mean that he was a hard man, though, and he gave Mike a warm smile before continuing with the funding meeting. Mike breathed a sigh of relief, thanking the stars that he wasn't the first academic who let his mind wander in an important meeting.

The truth was he hadn't had much sleep the previous night. It was only when he got back from dropping Amy Walsh home that the adrenaline rush of the fight finally hit him. He tried having a glass of milk but it was no good and he tossed and turned all night and not just because of the pain in his right hand. God, he hoped nobody noticed the nicks and scratches.

When he finally got up the next morning, all he could think about was what he'd got himself into, teaching Amy Walsh about the Arts. A part of him thought that the whole idea was crazy and wondered how the hell he'd let her talk him into it. But there was also another part of him that was increasingly nagging him. The part of him that wanted to stop Mad Jack before anyone else got hurt. He now knew where he was, but that simply wasn't good enough. He needed to know who he was if he was going to find him and Mike didn't have the faintest idea how to find that out, but Amy Walsh did. He needed her help as much as she needed his if he was going to have any hope of convincing Chris and Jon that the killer was a member of the Order.

Amy Walsh. God, why was her surname so familiar to him? It was a common name, of course, but he couldn't help feeling that he'd met another Walsh only recently and why was it bothering him so much?

He shook his head slightly and tried to concentrate, he was letting his mind wander again. He still thought that it was amazing that he'd got through his lunch break, let alone the two lectures and a tutorial he'd given that morning. The fact that he'd then managed to get through what was effectively a two-hour budget meeting in the afternoon was nothing short of a miracle.

Finally, the meeting ended and everyone seemed to simultaneously put their pens down and close their notebooks. "Uh, excuse me, Mike," Cookey asked just as Mike was standing up to leave, "can you stay behind for a moment, please? There's something I want to talk to you about."

"Uh, sure, Stuart." Mike sat back down, nervously wondering what this was about. He waited until everyone had left and Cookey closed the door behind them. "Um, is this about those exam papers? I mean I thought they were okay, I mean, please understand that it's my first time doing them…"

"Oh no, those papers were fine, Mike," Cookey said as he sat in the chair opposite him. "In fact, they were excellent."

Mike breathed a sigh of relief. "Oh, good. I'm glad to hear that."

Cookey smiled. "Now that I'm finally back in the office, I just wanted to see how you're getting on, after what happened last week."

Mike sighed again, but also found himself smiling slightly. Cookey had been in the States the previous week at a conference and therefore wasn't around when Kerry died. "Thanks, Stuart, I'm okay."

"I'm sorry about Kerry."

"Yeah, me too."

"Listen, I've managed to secure a bit of extra funding for some new library textbooks. I was thinking maybe we could include a dedication to Kerry in them."

"That… would be great. Can I just have one request, please?"

"Um, of course."

"I'd like to be the one who asks her parents."

Cookey nodded and smiled. "Certainly. I think that would be best." The two men stood up and shook each other's hand warmly. "If you need anything, Mike, just let me know. You know Graham and I are here for you if you need us."

"Thanks, Stuart, I appreciate that. How is Graham, by the way?"

"Oh fine. A lot better now that I'm back home. How's your mother?"

Mike smiled and told him she was fine, and they talked about personal things for a time before heading back to their respective offices.

When Mike got back to his, he sat down at his desk before breathing a heavy sigh. Looking over at the clock on the wall, he saw that it was nearly twenty past five. She'd be here soon. His lack of sleep was starting to catch up with him now and he was just about to put his head down on the desk for a quick five-minute snooze when his phone rang. He jolted upright and picked up the receiver. "Hello, Dr Michael Walker speaking."

"Hello, Dr Walker, this is reception. There's someone here to see you."

Oh, God, was she early?

"He says his name is Peter Simpkins and he's wondering if you could possibly spare him a few minutes?"

Simpkins? The Order's treasurer? What the hell could he want? Or maybe the correct question should be, what did Chris want? Well, there was only one way to find out. "Uh, yeah, tell him that I can literally spare five minutes if he'd like to come up now. Could you tell him where my office is please?"

"Of course, Dr Walker. I'll send him right up."

Mike checked the clock again. It was almost dead on twenty past now; he hoped he could make this quick. After what seemed like an eternity but couldn't have been more than two minutes, there was a nervous little knock on the door. "Come in, Mr Simpkins." Mike tried his best to sound cool and calm the way Jon always did but he was sure he failed.

The Order's treasurer cracked the door open ever so slightly and peered his head round. Mike nodded for him to come in and the short man gingerly stepped inside. He was wearing the same brown suit that he had on the previous day but with a yellow shirt and no robes. He was carrying a large leather bag in his left hand and the end of his staff was poking out of it. Mike gestured for him to pull up a chair before starting to question him. "What can I do for you, Mr Simpkins? And I'll warn you, please make it quick, I've only got five minutes and I'm expecting an important visitor."

"Really, sir, who?"

"None of your business! Now what the hell do you want?"

Simpkins gulped. "Oh, uh, yes, well, Sir, um..." He was clearly nervous and unsure about precisely what he was supposed to be doing there.

Mike realised that this was getting him nowhere and sighed. The only way he could move things on was to calm down and help Simpkins do the same. "Look, I'm sorry about last night. I didn't mean to burst in on your meeting with Chris like that but I'd had a bad day."

"Uh, yes, sir. I hope you... I mean, I hope I didn't get you into too much trouble with Keeper Rawlins?"

Mike smiled and chuckled slightly. "Oh, don't worry about Jon, I've had worse run-ins with him than that. Trust me; his bark's much worse than his bite."

Simpkins seemed to relax a little, he even gave a little smile. "I'm glad to hear that, sir, and may I just say that was a very impressive spell you used to, uh, open the vice-mage's door."

Mike couldn't help but smile himself and laugh. "Thanks. It's good to know I've still got it after being away for so long."

"Uh, yes, sir. Though I must say you seem to have done very well for yourself away from the Order." The little man gestured around the office. Mike got the impression that Simpkins was genuinely impressed.

"Thank you, I try." Curiosity got the best of him and he found himself asking, "Tell me, have you always been with the Order?"

"Oh yes, sir, I come from a long line; both my parents served with the keepers and my elder brother is actually the vice-mage of the South Yorkshire Chapter."

"Impressive."

Simpkins looked down. "I know what you're thinking, sir, and, uh, the truth is I've always been better with numbers than I have been with spells."

"Fair enough." Mike wasn't actually thinking that at all but he did sympathise; he knew all too well the pressures parents could put on their kids to do what they expected of them. Not from his own, of course, but he'd seen enough students who were forced to study science because they thought it was best for them that he knew what Simpkins was talking about. He considered giving some of the usual encouragement he gave to his students but realised the treasurer's problems were none of his business and decided to just press on. "We seem to have gone off on a bit of a tangent. What exactly can I do for you, Mr Simpkins? Like I say, I am expecting someone in a couple of minutes."

Again, Simpkins shuffled nervously but this time he answered the question. "Oh, uh, yes, well, um, Vice-Mage Saban was just wondering what made you consider that the Order could be involved in such horrible things as you were saying last night? Uh, whatever they may be!"

Mike leaned back for a moment, interlocking his fingers behind his head and mentally counting to 10. So that was it. Chris did have suspicions that what he'd told him yesterday could be true, but rather than have the keepers officially look into it, he was carrying out his own investigation and rather than soil his own hands to find out what he needed from Mike, he'd sent Simpkins to do his dirty work for him. The wily old fox. "I can assure you, Mr Simpkins, that you can tell Vice-Mage Saban that I had my reasons for getting as upset as I did and that if he wants to discuss them further with me himself, then he knows where to find me. Now, if you don't mind, I have an appointment at half—"

The phone rang again. "Excuse me. Yes, hello. Oh, excellent, Val. Could you ask her to just wait there and I'll be down in a minute? Cheers, thank you." He replaced the receiver and returned his attention to Simpkins. "That's my appointment now. So, if you don't mind, I have to go."

"Well, sir, if I could just ask…"

"I've already told you everything that I've got to say, Mr Simpkins. And like I say, I have to go." With that, he stood up and put on his jacket. Simpkins seemed a bit disappointed but he reluctantly stood up and followed Mike out the door and down the stairs.

Mike saw Amy Walsh waiting for him near the reception desk when they reached the ground floor. He waved to her and surprisingly she waved back. Mike hadn't realised the previous night just how attractive she truly was. She had on a a casual outfit of a baggy jumper and jeans set off with simple make-up and her long, curly brunette hair cascaded down to frame her pretty, young face perfectly. He hadn't realised how young she was either; she barely looked 24 but she must have been older to have a PhD. He suddenly felt that he needed a cold shower!

Amy had also had a hard time keeping her concentration at work that day. True, she was supposed to be working from home, but she just couldn't believe what she'd stumbled upon; a whole new world of wonder and secrets. Or had she? The sceptic in her couldn't help but still wonder if everything she'd seen was some sort of trick or that it had been due to the fact she was traumatised from being threatened with a knife. She shuddered slightly at the thought. No, it wasn't that, she knew better. What she'd seen last night was all too real and she had to find out more about it; how could she not? Who wouldn't want to find that there was more to life? She knew it was risky to look into this incredible new side of the world but it was so enticing, so seductive, that she just couldn't resist and also, most importantly, she finally had the break that would crack the case and stop Mad Jack. She could help Dave stop the killings and win both him and her brownie points with their respective superiors.

All she needed to do was get the information she needed from Michael Walker to complete her profile. The only thing was, could she trust him? He'd saved her life but she still knew nothing about him. Would he even give her the help she needed? If he was as powerful as he seemed, would she even be able to handle him?

Now, while standing by the School of Science and Technology's reception, she watched him come down the stairs. She hadn't noticed the night before how receding his hairline was, but she was still surprised how young he was. He must have been only in his early thirties at the most. Mind you, the grey polo neck jumper, blue jeans, white trainers and black leather jacket didn't exactly make him look mature. He was also quite plump. She wouldn't have said fat, but his round face certainly accentuated his size and reiterated her earlier view that he looked like some sort of nightclub bouncer. Still, he didn't look bad. In fact, she thought he looked quite, well, cuddly!

As he walked toward her, she flashed him a bright smile and offered him her hand to shake. "Hello, Dr Walker."

"Hi, Dr Walsh," he replied coolly as he shook it warmly.

He'd remembered her PhD! So few guys did that, but, then again, he did have one of his own! "Who's your friend?" she asked.

It was only then that Michael Walker seemed to notice that the short, balding man who had followed him down the stairs was still standing next to them. "He's just leaving," Mike stated simply.

The little man nodded apologetically and left. As he walked away, Amy couldn't help noticing the tip of what looked like a long piece of wood extending out of the bag he was carrying. She watched him go then looked sharply back at Michael Walker. "Was he a...?"

"Yes," he stated simply, "I'll tell you about it outside."

It was just as he led her out the door that she noticed the two female receptionists looking at them and whispering to each other. "Do they think we're...?"

"Yes."

She frowned slightly. "And you like that they do, don't you?"

This time he didn't answer, but he did blush, and Amy tried to fight back the smile that was forcing itself onto her face. At least, if nothing else, he was a typical man. That, she could handle!

Chapter 20

When they were safely outside of the university, Amy could tell that he'd relaxed a little and she felt that she could finally risk asking a few more questions. "So, does anyone know about your... abilities?"

He looked at her thoughtfully for a moment. "Excluding other magic-users?" She nodded. "In that case, just my mum."

She looked surprised. "But not your dad?"

"He's not around." He paused for a moment. "And I'd rather not talk about him."

"Oh, I'm sorry."

"That's okay."

"I'm the reverse." He gave her a surprised look. "I mean, my mum's gone. The big C."

"Oh, I see. I'm so sorry."

"Oh, don't worry about it. It's fine."

He gave her a sympathetic smile as he led her through the campus grounds toward the entrance of the university's multistorey car park.

"Must be handy having a free parking space in the town centre," she remarked conversationally.

"Oh, it's not free," he replied in a somewhat sarcastic tone. "I have to pay an annual fee for it."

"Say what? You're kidding, right?"

He shook his head. "Nope. It comes out of my salary every month and I have to justify it. Fortunately, since

I live in Redcar, I don't really have a problem as I can't exactly just jump on a bus to get here."

She shook her own head, and then suddenly thought of something else. "Hey, was your car parked here last night?"

He nodded. "Oh, yeah."

"So you carried me all the way to here?"

He squirmed slightly and looked a bit sheepish. "Well, not exactly. Technically speaking, I only held you while Kraven carried us."

"Kraven?"

"My familiar. The one I summoned last night to save you."

She took a moment to digest this and then her mouth dropped open. "Are you saying that we flew here?"

He gave her a sort of half-smile. "Well, yeah."

She looked away from him for a moment and tried to gather her thoughts. She got over the initial shock quite quickly and was amazed to discover that what annoyed her most wasn't that some weird creature had flown her through the night air, but that she hadn't been conscious to experience it!

By the time that she had calmed herself down, she found that she was already standing by the passenger side of Michael Walker's car and he was waiting at the driver's door, ready to open it, when he looked across the roof at her. She could tell he wanted to say something but seemed unsure, then he must have found the courage. "Listen, um, if we're gonna get to know each other, I mean, if I'm going to tell you things I've never really told anyone before..."

"Yes?"

"I was thinking maybe you could call me Mike?"

She looked at him in silence for a moment then replied, "On one condition."

"Name it."

"You call me Amy."

His face took on such a huge smile that she was sure it was going to split in two. "You've got a deal," he finally replied before unlocking the car and getting in.

As Amy slipped into the passenger seat, she asked him, "So where are we going?"

He looked at her awkwardly. "Well, I was thinking of either Roseberry Topping, as that's where I used to go to practise as a kid, or, if it's okay with you, we can just go back to my house."

Amy thought for a second. "I think that would be best, if you don't mind. I'm not sure I'm prepared for hill-climbing today."

"Fine with me," he said, before starting the engine and setting off.

They didn't really say much more during the journey as Mike drove them out of the town toward Redcar and they were soon pulling onto his driveway. Amy hadn't been paying much attention to the house the previous night, but now she got a good look at it in the light, she found herself both surprised and slightly disappointed. It was a normal and fairly new suburban three-bedroom detached house that looked pretty much like all the others on the estate. There were no gargoyles outside or even wind charms to ward off evil spirits. She also found herself thinking that she was probably in the wrong field and should have stuck with academia rather than going into the public service! Mind you, she did wonder if she would have kept such a nice house in as good condition as Mike Walker. As well as keeping the windows and guttering spotless, he also had the small front garden neatly trimmed and the few flowers that covered the edges were perfectly pruned.

Inside was a surprise, too; the house looked spotlessly clean and, again, all very normal. The banisters of the staircase were such a bright white that she half thought about shielding her eyes from them. The wood panel flooring was also bright and shiny. Again, she was struck by the lack of dark colours; all the walls were a warm oatmeal sort of colour and he even had a few pictures hung up on them. True, most of them were of various comic book and cartoon characters, but you couldn't have everything.

After taking their shoes off and hanging their jackets on the banister, Mike led her into the kitchen. Again, everything looked pristine: shiny granite-like worktops, oak-style wood units. A large window on the far wall showed a small back garden that was as neat and well kept as the one out the front.

"You have a very nice house," she found herself saying.

"Uh, thanks," he replied with an appreciative smile. "Um, would you like a cup of tea before we get started?"

"Depends – can you make it with magic?" she asked with a cheeky smile.

"If you like," he replied brightly.

Her eyes widened. "Are you serious? I mean, I was joking."

He smiled wryly. "How do you take your tea?"

"Uh, white and no sugar."

"Oh, same as me." With that, he snapped his fingers and the cupboards above him opened up and two cups flipped themselves out of it before floating down land gently on the counter. He then flicked his left wrist at the sink and she watched as the tap turned itself on and water poured from the spout. She waited expectantly for the kettle to lift itself up from the counter but he noticed where she was looking and shook his head before gesturing back to the running water. She watched in awe as the stream of water suddenly bent itself upward and flowed into the kettle. She stared in mild disbelief until suddenly he snapped his fingers. Almost instantaneously the tap turned off, the water stopped and the kettle switched itself on and started to boil. Amy couldn't help herself; she released a surprised gasp and started to clap her hands in applause. "Thank you," he said and gave a mock stage bow.

"That's incredible," she said. "You really can do magic. I mean, I knew you could, but to see it in front of me with my own eyes like that…"

He smiled. "Yeah, I had pretty much the same reaction the first time I saw it too."

"So how do you get this power?" she asked. "Is it like passed down through special bloodlines or something?"

He shook his head. "Nah, it's all just a matter of learning and a lot of practice. It's really just another skill that people can have but, like all things, some people are better at it than others. Oh, and before you ask, practising magic doesn't make you immortal either. Your average wizard or witch won't live any longer than anyone else and we're just as likely to get sick from anything, like a cold, as you are."

She raised her eyebrows. "Fair enough. I take it wizards are men and witches are women."

He chuckled as he poured the hot water into the cups. "I was waiting for you to ask that one. No, that's not true either. There's a distinct difference between witchcraft and wizardry and it has nothing to do with gender. Witchcraft tends to be taught in families as part of various religions, such as Wicca. Whereas wizards tend to form Orders and teach their craft from a master to an apprentice and are part of other religions, like Christianity. Is this strong enough for you, by the way?" he said, indicating to one of the cups of tea that he was making. She nodded and let him carry on as he threw away the tea bags in a nearby peddle bin. "Also, witches generally draw their power from this world while wizards draw their power from the next world," He continued as he retrieved a two-pint carton of semi-skimmed milk from the fridge. "Let me know what's enough for you," he said as he started pouring it into the cups.

"Uh, yeah, that's fine. Thank you." She accepted the cup of tea gratefully and took a sip as he returned the milk to the fridge. "Uh, what exactly do you mean by power from the next world? Lovely cup of tea, by the way."

He flashed her another smile and picked up his own cup. "Thanks. It's probably better if I show you. Come with me upstairs."

She stood still, staring at him. It was only when he got to the doorway that he turned around and said, rather embarrassed, "Sorry, I mean that's where I have my lab."

She pretended to breathe another sigh of relief and then giggled at him. It was only when she'd followed him halfway up the stairs that he realised she was teasing him!

Chapter 21

Mike led Amy up the stairs and into one of the two back bedrooms of the property, though bedroom was probably not the correct descriptive term for it anymore. Amy guessed that it was probably the larger of the two spare rooms; he'd called it a lab but she thought it looked more like a study. There was a desk with a laptop in one corner, as well as a writing pad with pens and other paraphernalia. Two of the walls contained simple flat-pack bookshelves that looked like they were ready to collapse under the weight of the books they were filled with. She noticed that one of them was filled completely with scientific textbooks. She couldn't help but wonder what the other one was filled with. Whatever they were, they seemed to be all large hardbacks and, from what she could see of the spines, had no dust covers and were covered in weird symbols.

"So, uh, what exactly do you research in here?" she asked. "I mean, do you only research physics nowadays or do you still keep your hand in magic?"

Mike looked over at her and bit his lower lip. "Honestly?" She nodded. "Well, officially, at the university, my research interests are new mathematical models of string theory."

Amy had no idea what he was talking about but she nodded her head before saying, "Okay. And unofficially?"

He paused again before continuing. "I'm trying to find the link between science and magic!"

Her eyes widened. "The link?"

He rubbed the bridge of his nose with his left hand. "How do I explain it? Let's start with what you know about science."

She made a face. "Well, that won't take long. To say I wasn't a fan when I was at school would be an understatement."

"OK, but what do you know? Like what are the three main sciences?"

She smiled. "That one, I can answer. There's biology, chemistry and the one you teach, physics."

"Yeah, that's right. Can you think of anything that they all seem to have in common? I mean, if you think of them in very broad terms."

Amy whistled through her teeth. "Well biology is the study of living things, right? Uh, chemistry is the study of chemical structure, I think, and physics is the study of matter, isn't it?"

"Pretty broad, but that's the sort of thing I'm looking for. Can you see what they, sort of, all have in common?"

Amy thought for a minute. "They all deal with physical things?"

Mike smiled and clicked his fingers before pointing at her. "Exactly. They're fundamentally all about studying the physical aspects of the universe. They allude to energies and forces that act upon them, but they don't define them too clearly."

Suddenly Amy realised what he was getting at. "But magic is the study of these energies and forces and how they can be used to act on matter?"

"Exactly. Now, these energies and forces come in a variety of forms, they flow all around us and through us. There's energy that flows though the world, like gravity, electricity and magnetism. Witchcraft calls the flow of these energies 'lay lines' and teaches its practitioners how to manipulate them in order to perform their spells. You see, witches use their wands to control the flow of lay lines and bend these natural powers to their will. That's what gives them their power."

Amy nodded thoughtfully. "Okay that's all very well and interesting, but what about wizards? I mean, that's really what I need to know, right?"

Mike smiled. "Yeah, fair enough. Well, like I said, wizards draw their power from what they call the next world."

"What they call the next world?"

"Well, actually, most of them call it the spirit world. But don't panic, it's not what you think. It's basically another dimension that's parallel to this one, or maybe more like at right angles to it. It's not like this world, it's sort of intangible, like pure energy, but it bleeds into this one and it's possible to harness its power and store it to be released later."

"Okay, but how does that work? I mean, what do they store it in...?" Suddenly, she thought back to the previous night and realised the answer herself before he had chance to reply. "The staff!" she screamed, nearly spilling what was left of her tea. "So that's why it's the source of his power!"

"You're catching on."

"But how do you store power in a staff? I mean, how do you access the spirit world?"

126

He frowned slightly and rubbed his hand over his mouth. "Maybe it would be best if I showed you."

He walked over to another corner of the room that contained a small, locked cabinet. He flicked his hand at it and the door swung open with a satisfying click. Placing his now empty cup on top of the cabinet, he reached into it and produced two items; one was a rolled-up black cloth, the other was a thin black rod, no more than two feet long and an inch in diameter. A large, perfectly clear gem had somehow been attached to one end of the rod; if Amy didn't know better, she would have sworn that it was a diamond! Mike noticed her staring and gave her a half smile. "It was a present from my father when I joined the Order." He shrugged and gave a strange sound, half sigh, half 'humph', before saying, "It's ironic, really; it's the only thing I have left from him and I don't even use it now."

She gave him an apologetic smile; for some reason this seemed to perk him up a bit. Then she asked, "No offence intended but you know last night with Mad Jack? Well, I can't help but notice that well…"

"That my staff's a lot smaller than his was?"

"Well, yes." She tried to keep a straight face but couldn't help herself and started to giggle. "I'm sorry," she said and started to laugh uncontrollably. It later struck her how crazy it was to laugh about the innuendo of something that nearly killed her.

Suddenly, she realised that he was laughing as well. He waited until they'd both calmed down before continuing. "It's all right, I know what you mean. But the size," he said, raising his eyebrows, "isn't the only indication of how much power a staff will hold. The type of material and any additions, such as this," he continued, tapping the diamond, "can all assist with both storage and discharge of its power." He held the staff up to her. "Would you hold this for a minute for me please?"

She looked at him blankly. "Uh, are you sure?"

He gave a slight laugh. "Of course. Don't worry, I promise it won't bite!"

Continuing to grip the teacup in her right hand, she gingerly extended her left one and wrapped her fingers around the staff. It felt cool and smooth, like highly polished wood. She suddenly realised that that was probably exactly what it was. The more she looked at it, the more she thought that what it actually appeared to be was one of those old-fashioned gentlemen's canes. It was only when Mike released his own grip on it that she noticed how heavy the diamond was on the tip. If it was real, God only knew what it was worth! Despite this, she found herself to be disappointed to find that the staff felt very, well, ordinary. She shook it in her hand slightly but it just felt like an ordinary, albeit slightly top-heavy, cane. She started to wonder what exactly she'd been expecting; maybe that it would feel electrically charged or something.

While she was examining the staff, Mike was unrolling the black cloth out onto the floor. It was then that she noticed that it had an ornately decorated white pattern on it in the centre. It seemed to consist of a large circle, maybe a metre or so in diameter. Six points were evenly marked on the circle and joined up to form a star. Each of the six small triangles that made up the star contained a different symbol, none of which Amy had ever seen before. Some seemed to resemble mythical creatures like dragons and others looked like nothing more than odd collections of geometrical shapes. A seventh symbol, a spiral that wound down to a central point, was in the dead centre of the star. After he'd padded down the edges so that the cloth was completely flat, he walked over to the window and drew the curtains. "Don't want to spook the neighbours," he said as he took the staff from her.

Amy was starting to get a bit nervous now. Although she liked to consider herself liberal, the thought of the pagan-like symbols disturbed her stern Catholic upbringing slightly. She gripped her teacup and watched silently as he took the staff and struck it into the dead centre of the spiral and stood back. Amy was amazed to see that the staff remained upright and didn't fall over. She was so busy trying to see if he'd pierced the cloth and jammed it into the floor that she didn't notice that he'd slowly started to pace around the cloth in a continuous circle. When she looked up, she also noticed that he was waving his hands in a series of movements to form complex patterns in the air.

He continued doing this for what seemed like five minutes and she was just about to ask how much longer this was going to take, when it happened. It started off slowly. The air around the staff seemed to distort and quiver almost as if she was looking at it through mist or even water. Then a spark like a bolt of lightening flashed between the diamond on the cane and one of the corners of the star on the cloth. It was so fast that Amy wondered if she'd just imagined it, then there was another from one of the other points, then another, and another. Then another appeared but this one was larger, brighter and accompanied by a loud crackle like thunder. Then another like it appeared, but this time it didn't disappear, the bright white stream of electricity crackled loudly and clearly, connecting the star point to the diamond. Then, almost immediately, another permanently appeared from one of the other points, then another and another until finally six bolts of bright, white electricity flashed between the points of the star and the diamond handle.

Amy stood there transfixed at the incredible sight; suddenly she was acutely aware of the power radiating from the reams of energy. It wasn't warm or anything, in fact she didn't feel it on her face or skin at all; it was just there almost as if it was in her very soul. She found herself reaching for her crucifix and held it tightly with her right hand. Like always, it comforted her and she no longer felt the power of the energy. Suddenly, Mike made a dramatic sweeping gesture with his arms and almost immediately the electricity vanished and the staff fell to one side on top of the cloth.

She looked up at him sharply and he pointed at her chest. "Is that a cross or a crucifix or something?" he asked suddenly.

She was startled. Oh God, what was wrong? Maybe he hated religion or maybe just her religion. Was she in danger? What should I say? No, she refused to be intimidated, especially about her faith. "Yes, it's a crucifix. Why?"

He clapped his hands and pointed at her again. "Of course, so that's it!" His voice wasn't angry; in fact, Amy thought he sounded... excited.

"What's it?" she asked.

"That's why he couldn't enthral you!"

* * *

He gave one last almighty tug and the zip finally went past the kink and closed before breaking off and embedding itself in his left index finger. He swore under his breath and threw the offending bit of metal into the corner of the room. Even the disposal of this one was proving difficult. He stood there for a moment, sucking his finger and cursing. Now the question begged, where to get rid of this one?

Chapter 22

Amy stared at her crucifix as she held its chain in her hand and let it dangle below her palm. She was sitting on the same two-seater sofa in Michael Walker's lounge that she'd found herself laying on the previous evening. He was currently in the kitchen making them something to eat for dinner.

"So," she yelled out to him, "you really think that this saved my life?"

"Not exactly," he yelled back, "hang on, I'm nearly finished."

It wasn't long before he entered, carrying a plate containing what he said was his own version of chicken Parmigiana. She didn't like to say that she'd never heard of it before, but it seemed to be a chicken breast cooked in a tomato-based marinade, topped with Parmesan cheese and, if nothing else, it certainly smelt good!

She'd offered to help him make dinner but he insisted he was fine, so she accepted his offer to take a break and gather her thoughts about what she'd seen and been told. A small part of her had thought that maybe she should keep an eye on what he was doing, but a larger part of her had realised that, if he had wanted to harm her, not only could he have done it by now but he almost certainly had the power to do something a lot more subtle than drug her food!

She put her crucifix back on over her head and took the plate off him with a polite 'thank you' before resting it on her lap. She waited until he returned with his own plate and seated himself in the easy chair opposite her before starting to eat.

"Uh, what do you think?" he asked hopefully.

She finished chewing the tender piece of chicken she was currently enjoying and smiled. "It's very nice. Thank you very much." He again gave that broad smile that she now knew meant he was genuinely chuffed. She suddenly realised that she really liked that smile, it was sweet. "So, how did my crucifix save me?" she asked.

"Like I said, technically speaking, it didn't. The Higher Power did."

"Sorry?"

"What most people call God!"

She stopped eating and stared at him. "Say what?"

"You sound surprised. But you must believe in order for it to have worked." Now she was puzzled. "Sorry, let me explain. Well, at least as best as I can. You see, not even the most powerful and knowledgeable wizards understand this completely but there is a power greater than both this world and the spirit world. Very little is understood about it, but it can certainly influence events both here and in the spirit world. It seems to have the power to literally switch magic off. It provides protection to people who have strong faith through religious artefacts and symbols, as well as holy ground."

"So it could be an intelligent supreme being like we believe?" Amy asked excitedly.

Mike gave a wry smile. "Well speaking as a religious man myself, I certainly like to think so."

"Are you Catholic too?"

He shook his head. "Church of England."

"Fair enough." She smiled for a moment and bit her lower lip slightly before eating another piece of chicken.

He waited until she finished chewing then decided to ask some questions of his own. "So how does one end up becoming a criminal profiler?"

She gave a sort of muted chuckle and shrugged. "Fighting against tradition, I suppose."

"I'm not sure I'm following you."

"Well, as the old cliché goes, it's a long story."

"That's okay, I've got time," he said with a slight laugh. "As long as you don't mind telling me."

She smiled. "No, of course not. Well, as I said before, my mum died when I was young. Dad was a copper, so he didn't really have much time for me, so I was more or less raised by my older sister, who's now a barrister."

"And you didn't want to follow in either of their footsteps?"

She sighed. "Sort of." Her voice sounded heavy, like a mixture of regret and bad memories. Mike himself was intimately familiar with both. "To be perfectly honest, me and her didn't really get on too well. I think she resented that she was made to look after me and, if I'm honest, I resented that she thought she could take Mum's place. I also had the usual chip on my shoulder that the youngest always has, in that I got no responsibility and everyone bossed me around. Which was made worse by the fact that our dad trusted our brother to pretty much do whatever he liked because he was a boy, even though he was only a few years older than me!" She said the last part so fast and with such conviction that Mike got the impression that she'd repeated it many times before. He couldn't help but wonder how much of it was to convince others and how much it was just to convince herself.

"So you decided to go down a different path to your family and study psychology?"

"More or less. I still inherited the family sense of wanting to make a difference, though. When I first started, I wanted to be a clinical psychologist, y'know, help people with mental health problems, stuff like that, but I found I was better at studying behaviours and predicting patterns. Then when I got offered a PhD down South studying criminal behaviour, I decided I should just give up and accept the inevitable and be a criminal profiler."

"Can't say that I see that as accepting defeat. It sounds like an important job to me and I bet it's not easy to get into."

She chuckled. "Thanks. I suppose that's true and I do like the fact that what I do is important and... Oh my God."

Mike looked up sharply from eating his last piece of chicken. "What's wrong?"

"Is that the time?"

He glanced over at his wall clock to see that it read nine thirty. Where on Earth had the time gone?

"I've got to get home so I can get to work on my profile." She stood up and carried her plate into the kitchen. Mike reluctantly got up and followed her. When he reached the kitchen, she was already rinsing her plate down in the sink. "Thanks to what you've shown and told me, I'm sure I can expand the profile now to explain some of the problems."

Mike looked at her with a growing sense of disappointment; the time had passed so quickly. It had been so long since he'd had the chance to spend this much time with someone and be so honest about himself with them. Not having to hide who and what he was all the time was just so great and he suddenly realised how much he didn't want it to end, especially with her. There was something about Amy Walsh. He really enjoyed her company. "So, uh, does this mean you don't need me to tell you anything else?"

She stopped dead and looked up at him. "Well, uh, I mean, is there anything more to tell?"

He thought for a moment. "Well, there are other types of evocations and…" He paused. And what? Then he thought of something, but could he tell her that? It was risky, but… Oh, to hell with it. "I could maybe tell you something about the structure of the Order. Maybe that would help."

She suddenly smiled brightly. God, her smile was amazing. Mike knew it was another cliché but her smile literally did light up the room. "Yeah, please, if you could. That would be really useful."

"I hoped it might be."

"Sorry?"

"Oh, I mean I thought it might be!"

He lugged the heavy duffel bag into the boot of his car and slammed the door shut. He still had no idea where to take this one. Well, it would be safe in there for now. He stretched his arms and gave a loud yawn. He'd deal with it tomorrow, it wasn't important now. It was time to get back and enjoy his prizes.

Mike drove Amy back round to her flat in little under half an hour. It wasn't a difficult route so he remembered it quite well from the previous night. When he pulled up outside the entrance she turned to him and gave him an awkward, nervous smile. "Um, please don't think I'm rude," she said, "I really would like to invite you in for a drink but from the look of the light that's on in my lounge window, I think my flatmate's still up."

Mike shrugged. He honestly hadn't even thought about being invited into her flat, but now that she'd mentioned it, he felt a strange mix of pride and disappointment all at once. Still, he found himself saying, "It's all right. I understand."

She nodded and unbuckled her seat belt. She was just about to open the car door when she stopped dead. Suddenly she spun around and kissed him on the cheek. "Thank you," she said with that amazing 'light up the room' smile. "I'll see you on Saturday." With that, she swiftly exited the vehicle.

Mike just sat there and watched her close the car door. He found himself raising his arm and waving as she reached the flats' entrance and this time she did stop to turn and wave back at him before entering the building.

It was only as he was driving out of the estate that he realised a grin had appeared on his face and that he'd all but completely forgotten about the scrapes on his hand.

He started to wonder if maybe Amy Walsh had been lying about not knowing any magic herself. It certainly felt like she'd cast a spell on him!

Chapter 23

"Look, I am not going to stand here and be insulted!"

"There's no need to shout, David."

Dave turned toward Chief Inspector Williams and gave a clearly audible snarl. The smug git was going too far. "Now you listen to me…"

"That's enough, Dave." Detective Superintendent Nick Shaw's voice was firm and final; Dave stopped silent and stood glowering at Williams. The weeks of fake civility he had been putting on with the chief inspector from London had all come crashing down in the last few minutes and to make matters worse, it had been slap bang in the middle of his superior's office! At least there was only the three of them there. Nothing would have been worse than having his subordinates see him lose his temper like that, especially Jenny, uh, Sergeant Granger.

After about 10 seconds of heavy breathing, Superintendent Shaw continued. "Chief Inspector Williams, I wish to apologise for my colleague's outburst." Dave stiffened but remained silent. Shit, this was it. "However, I understand Inspector Walsh's frustration. This is not your patch and you would do well to remember that!"

Williams smiled and gave a polite nod. "Of course, sir, I'm sorry." He then turned toward Dave. "I do apologise, Inspector."

For about half a second, Dave considered telling him where to shove his apology, but he quickly realised that would mean bye-bye, career. "Yes, well. I'm sorry too, Chief Inspector, my outburst was uncalled for." He tried to keep as much of the sarcasm out of his voice as possible but he was sure he'd failed.

Superintendent Shaw shook his head slightly. He was a short man, barely regulation height for the police force, with thinning white hair. He had a reputation for being a cranky old school copper but Dave had long ago learnt that his rough appearance hid a mind like a steel trap. As well as being a brilliant detective, he was also an excellent administrator and was fiercely protective of his team, a fact that Dave hoped he was now about to demonstrate.

Shaw looked up at Williams again slowly and deliberately before finally continuing. "Now, Inspector Williams, I do value your assistance and input in this case, I mean, I'm the first to agree with you that our area has not had the greatest experience with serial killers. However, I do not appreciate being told that we do not know how to run an investigation." Williams looked like he was about to say something but the Superintendent cut him off before he could get a word in. "And I don't care if that wasn't what you meant. That was what was inferred and I don't appreciate it. Now, if you don't mind, I'd like to speak with Inspector Walsh alone for a moment."

The expression on Williams's face didn't change and he merely replied, "As you wish, sir." He turned to Dave and gave a polite nod. "Inspector." Dave didn't give a response and Williams didn't wait for one; he just turned and left.

Dave breathed a small sigh of relief under his breath but he knew better than to feel smug or count his chickens yet; he'd still really screwed up and there were going to be consequences. He turned his attention back to his boss. The superintendent was now sat with his elbows on his desk, with his face leaning against his hands, looking at Dave intently. His hands were clasped together with his fingers perfectly straight; it almost looked like he was praying. Dave wondered if maybe he was asking God for patience.

Finally, Shaw spoke. "That was stupid, David!"

"Yeah, I know, sir."

"I know how frustrating this situation is but losing your temper is not going to help."

"Yes, sir."

"And whether you like it or not, Williams has got a point. The only reason that you're leading this investigation is because you had the good, or maybe that should be bad, luck to be given the case of the first victim." Dave didn't answer that one. Shaw didn't lose any more of his temper but, then again, he did seem to have very little of it left to lose. "I mean, do you have any idea what sort of pressure we're under?"

"Yes, sir."

"Do you? The town's in a state of panic. People are afraid to go out at night. This is even making the national news now. Did you know that the mayor actually came down in person to find out exactly what I was doing about this situation?" Dave remained silent; he could hear the anger entering the superintendent's voice now and was starting to get nervous. Shaw sighed. "Look, Dave, what I'm saying is we're all getting stressed to breaking point. Do you want to be removed from this case?"

"No, sir, of course not."

"Are you sure? Maybe I should take Williams's advice and have a more experienced officer take over."

"Oh, come on, sir. You know bloody well how much I've worked my arse off on this case trying to catch this bastard…"

"Yeah, 'trying' being the operative word!"

"We will get him!"

"Are you sure? Or are you still just wanting to prove something?"

"What's that supposed to mean, sir?"

Shaw sighed. "Look, I know your dad was a great copper and that retirement didn't suit him…"

"This has nothing to do with my father."

"Hasn't it?"

"No!"

Shaw took a deep breath and let it out slowly. "It better not be, Dave, that's all I'm saying. Look, just get out there and find this guy." Dave nodded and headed to the door. He was just reaching for the handle when Shaw shouted after him, "Dave!" He looked back. "I can't cover your back forever without results." He nodded and walked out.

Detective Sergeant Granger looked down sharply at the report on her desk as the superintendent's door swung open again and the inspector stepped out. Was this it? Was it all over? She'd already seen Williams leave the super's office a short time earlier. She couldn't tell whether he was in a good mood or not. But, then again, she never could tell what mood Williams was ever in; his face always seemed to be an expressionless mask to her. It was like he was constantly laughing at a private joke that nobody else in the world was privy to, but at the same time was too composed and professional to let anyone see he was enjoying it.

Jenny was really worried now. She knew that they couldn't keep this up forever; they were literally getting nowhere. They had no leads and few to zero clues. If they didn't have a break soon, someone would have to take the case off them if just to show the media that they were doing something. If she was being honest, she wouldn't mind moving on to something else; this case was becoming too intense. It was eating into every aspect of their lives and the inspector was becoming obsessed. Still, she couldn't bear the thought of how crushed Dave, uh, Inspector Walsh, would be if they lost the case.

As he came over and sat down at the desk opposite her, Jenny couldn't help but become even more worried. He looked worn out and dejected. Trying to appear cool and casual, she looked up and gave him a slight smile. "Hi, sir."

"Hi, Sarge," was all he said. His expression was blank. Not grim, just blank. He sat there staring at nothing in particular as if he was unable to focus on anything. Jenny was about to risk asking if he was okay when finally he spoke again. "Have forensics come back with their full report yet on the last victim?"

"Uh, yes, sir."

"And?"

She sighed. "Same as the others, I'm afraid, sir. Nothing at all. Toxicology was blank, there were no drugs or anything in her system, yet she seemed to put up no resistance while he just... Well, butchered her."

"And SOCO?"

"The same – nothing. No fingerprints, no DNA, nothing left at the crime scene except the duffel bag her body was in." The inspector bowed his head and rubbed his fingers through his hair. Jenny couldn't bear to see him like this. "Uh, your sister called, sir." Maybe this would cheer him up.

"Oh yeah?" was his unenthusiastic reply.

"She says she thinks she's nearly got the profile figured out."

"Oh yeah?" he repeated, but he didn't look up. "Go on then, what did she say about him that we don't already know?"

Jenny squirmed slightly in her chair; maybe this had been a mistake. "Uh, well, she said it wasn't quite finished yet and that she didn't want to give it to you until it was complete. But she wanted to let you know that there were only a couple of things that she still needed to check. And she did say that she's got it all in hand and is going to get the last of the information tomorrow and she should have the profile ready for Monday."

"Right," was all Dave said.

Jenny nodded slightly and looked back down at the report. Well, that went well. All she could do now was hope against hope that Amy could bring them some sort of miracle.

He drove the car out toward the large blue structure slowly and carefully. This was the first time he'd carried out a disposal during the daylight and he was enjoying every minute of it. He had considered waiting for the night but he was getting sick of the same monotonous procedure over and over again. It was time to push his limits further and prove to himself what he could do.

He'd made careful preparations, ensuring that his staff had been fully charged and started the incantation before he'd even set off. He'd driven out of the town centre toward the industrial area, and then, just as he took the slip road, he completed the spell and released the energy in the staff. He then manipulated and controlled the power to pull it round the car in the best veil he had ever created. He was now completely invisible to the eyes of the unenlightened and he drove the rest of the way in quiet confidence.

He brought the car to a smooth, silent stop at the base of the structure. He was relieved to see that the area was as deserted as he was expecting. He picked up his staff and exited his vehicle. He kept an infusion of his will within the length of timber to ensure that both he and the car remained invisible to the naked eye of the unenlightened. True, one of his peers might have been able to detect something but none of them would be interested in coming here.

He popped the car's boot open and removed the duffel bag before carrying it to the base of the structure. He tossed it down next to the nearest steel support before walking back to his car. He removed the bag of white powder from his jacket pocket, muttered the incantation 'Nifalto, unfino' under his breath and watched as the dust cloud wiped away his footprints and anything else he'd left in his wake. In no time at all, it was done.

He kept the veil up as he headed back into the car and started to hum cheerfully under his breath. It was time to go back and view his prizes.

Chapter 24

Mike drove up to the building that contained Amy's flat and parked in one of the designated spaces that were marked for visitors. He found himself swallowing a yawn. Once again, he'd failed to get much sleep the previous night and had suffered with more than a bit of difficulty in keeping his concentration at work over the last couple of days. But at least the soreness in his hand had gone now and the cuts had all but healed up.

Amy had invited him to come over to her flat just before lunch on Saturday. She'd said her flatmate was working on the morning so they wouldn't be disturbed and she could finally give him the cup of tea that she owed him before they went out. They'd agreed to go to Roseberry Topping, where Mike had promised to show her more magic. He wasn't sure exactly what this meant for them, but his excited mind was still trying to process the fact that she had given him her mobile number, not to mention taken his!

He looked over at the small, plain, wooden box he'd brought with him that was laying on the passenger seat. It was actually an old jewellery box that had once belonged to his grandmother. His mum had let him have it years ago for keeping some of his magical gear in. He really wanted to do something to impress Amy and also maybe hint at how much he liked her and he thought that what he'd got in the box might enable him to do just that. He'd been mentally preparing himself for this moment all morning, but now that he was finally here, he was incredibly nervous. Was this really the best thing to do? It might impress her but... But what? He smiled to himself. What the hell? He had nothing to lose, and so much to gain. He grabbed the box and got out before he had a chance to change his mind again.

The flats that Amy Walsh lived in seemed to be an interesting mix to Mike. Although they were clearly brand new, made in that sandstone-coloured brick that all the home builders seemed to be using nowadays, the fact that they were only three stories high and contained only six flats (two on each floor) made them look, well, quaint. Mike pressed the buzzer for flat 3.1 and waited with bated breath.

After a few seconds, he heard Amy's slightly distorted voice say, "Hello."

"Hi, uh, yeah, it's me, Mike."

"Yeah, come on up."

He heard a buzzing sound followed by a click from the main door. It swung open with a slight scuff of the carpet as he let himself in. The first thing he noticed was that there was no lift; he wondered for a second how the developers had managed to get round the building health and safety regulations before trotting up the stairs and knocking nervously on flat 3.1. It took less than a second for the door to open and again he smelt that amazing wild flower and honey perfume as Amy appeared in the doorway.

"Hi, come on in." She was wearing a plain pink tee shirt with red tracksuit bottoms that bore the emblem of Middlesbrough Football Club. She stood to one side to let him pass.

While she was locking the door, Mike took the opportunity to have a quick look around the flat. There was no hallway; the door opened up into a small lounge area that seemed to be a perfect square shape, with a lone two-seater settee, an oak wood coffee table and a flatscreen television. A thin strip of a kitchenette lined one wall and three doors that Mike assumed led to the bedrooms and bathroom lined the other. With the exception of the two small windows, the remaining two walls were covered with pictures, most showing Amy and lots of other people partying and having fun. Mike wasn't surprised to find that she was popular but he still felt a little pang of jealousy. He wondered who in the photographs was her flatmate but his thought was interrupted.

"I hope these will be okay?" Amy asked, indicating the tracksuit bottoms. "I'm not really into hill-walking so I don't really have any mountaineering clothes. So I was thinking of just wearing these with a heavy coat."

"Oh, don't worry; I've got no proper mountain gear either," Mike said with a smile. "I usually just wear jeans and a jumper when I go."

Amy smiled back; Mike thought his knees were going to turn to jelly. "Unfortunately, all my jeans are all in the wash at the moment," she said, "so I'll have to settle for these."

"Are you a fan?" Mike asked, pointing out the football club's emblem.

Amy frowned slightly. "Not really, these were a present from my dad. To be perfectly honest, I don't really follow football."

"That's all right, neither do I." She laughed. "So how's the profile coming along?"

"Oh, very well, thanks. I think I'm starting to get a real sense of the killer now, but I also feel that I'm still missing the last little bit."

"Anything I can help with?"

"Hopefully. I think what I need is an idea about what sort of social circle he'd move in."

"Well, maybe a bit of info on the Order might help."

"Excellent, I'm looking forward to hearing it. Uh, listen, I wanted to return the favour for the meal you cooked the other night but I was hoping we could get away as soon as possible. So I hope you don't mind but I've just made us some sandwiches to eat later while we're out."

"Oh, that's fine."

"Are you sure? Um, would you like a cup of tea or coffee before we go?"

"Yeah, tea please. Er, actually, before we go, there's something I'd like to show you, if it's okay?"

She'd already started to boil the kettle and get the cups out. "Uh, okay. What?" He came over to her and placed the box on the kitchen counter beside her. "What's that?" she asked. Mike opened the box and took out a handful of fine brown granules and let them fall through his fingers back into the wooden container. She gave him a puzzled frown. "Sand? What's that for?"

He smiled. "I thought maybe you'd be sick of watching me do magic and might like to try some yourself."

She stared at him for a moment as the kettle boiled. "Sorry? Say what?"

"Do you trust me?" She didn't answer him and just stood there, open-mouthed. Mike stepped toward her and took both her hands in his own; they felt cool and as smooth as silk. For a moment, their eyes met and

Mike felt like he could lose himself from looking into them; they were a wonderful deep brown, wide-eyed and innocent, but also passionate and warm.

He mentally shook himself down and forced himself to concentrate. He needed to be completely composed to do this. He brought her hands together and asked her to make a cup with them. He then picked up the box and poured the sand into her palms before replacing it on the counter top. "I told you how witchcraft uses the power of Earth and that wizardry uses the power of the spirit world, but there is another power that I didn't mention."

"What's that?" she asked nervously.

"The power of the soul. The power within ourselves. What's called sorcery." She looked up at him sharply and he tried to give her a reassuring smile. "Before I show you this, do you know what sand is made of?"

"Uh, silica, isn't it?"

"Spot on. And do you know what glass is made of?"

"That's silica as we— What? No way!" She looked down at her cupped hands to see the sand still resting within it.

Mike grinned slightly. "Can I take your crucifix off for a minute?"

She seemed to think about it for a second but said, "Um, yeah, okay."

Mike reached out and gently unhooked the chain around her neck and placed the necklace on the table next to the box. He then placed his own hands over hers, making sure that his psychic defences were properly up. "Would you close your eyes for me please?" She bit her lip slightly but did as he asked; he then closed his as well.

Amy felt the sand in her hands and between her fingers. It was rough and course like little pieces of grit. Then she felt Mike's hands cover hers; they felt warm and soft. Although she was nervous, she couldn't help but giggle slightly. He asked her to try to be silent and to look within herself. She had no idea what he meant. Then he asked her to concentrate on her hands but not from the outside, to look from within. She still didn't understand what he was saying, but tried to imagine what was beneath her skin, beneath the flesh; she tried to imagine her skeleton and then tried to trace her way through it toward her hands. She tried to imagine looking through her hands to the sand and…

"Oh my God," she exclaimed. She felt it. She could sense something emanating from her hands; she could feel energy. She didn't know where it was coming from but she could sense it radiating from her palms.

"That's it," he said calmly. "Try and hold onto that."

She found herself doing as he said and held on to the feeling of that power, then she started to feel something else creeping in. Suddenly, she realised that it was power radiating from his hands that was carefully making its way into her own. "Please don't be afraid," he asked softly.

"I'm not." She later wondered whether she was more surprised by the fact that she said that or by the fact that she meant it. She felt his power mix into hers then she felt her own power reach out from her hands and clasp around the sand like a pair of invisible fists, crushing and compacting it. Suddenly, she realised what was happening; he was using his own power to guide hers. She was doing magic! He was just showing her how.

Something else was starting to happen now; she felt her power being guided to further pressurise and shape the sand in some way by rotating it like a small cyclone. She couldn't tell what was happening exactly, but she felt the sand start to warm up. It didn't get white hot, just pleasantly warm. Then, after about a minute, she felt his power retract and her own snapped back suddenly into its original state. She was so shocked that she opened her eyes and gasped.

"Are you okay?" he asked.

"Uh, yeah," she replied. "That was incredible." He smiled and looked down at their hands. She followed his gaze and watched him remove his hands from hers to reveal that she was now holding a perfectly smooth, sparkling, crystal clear gem. She looked back up at him. "Is this a...?"

He smiled warmly and shook his head. "I'm afraid not. It's just glass. What you've just done is taken the base elements of the sand and rearranged them into a different structure. It's what's known as alchemy."

Amy looked down at the glass jewel and turned it around in her fingers. She closed her eyes to see if she could feel that power again. She did what she'd done before and imagined her skeleton and imagined looking through it and there it was. She hadn't imagined it, but, try as she might, she just couldn't bend and shape it like Mike could. She opened her eyes and looked at the glass gem again in slight frustration.

Mike laughed. "Sorry, but I'm afraid it's not that easy. It takes a lot of practise and training to control your energy like that." She looked up and gave him a sharp stare. "Uh, sorry, I didn't mean that you can't do it, I just mean that you need time to learn, and someone needs to teach you. I mean, there is a technique to it."

He stared at her and gulped, but her look softened and she gave him that warm smile again and laughed slightly. "That's okay. Thank you for sharing that with me. I think it counts as one of the most amazing experiences of my life."

She offered him the glass gem but he shook his head. "No, please, I'd like you to keep it."

"Are you sure?"

"Positive."

She held it in her fist for a moment and bit her lip. "Thank you so much," she said with a smile. "I'll keep it with me in my purse for good luck."

Mike was sure his heart skipped a beat as she picked her crucifix back up.

152

Chapter 25

Kevin Turner knew that he was pushing his luck as he walked up to his ex-girlfriend's flat but he really didn't care. He'd always been a great believer in the old adage, 'nothing ventured, nothing gained.' He knew Amy had to have some info on how the Mad Jack investigation was going and if he could just get close enough to her and turn on the old Turner charm, he could wheedle out the details about how well her brother's investigation was going. It also meant an excellent opportunity to get close to her again and rekindle the old flame. He just had to make her realise how important the press' involvement was in this case. You can't keep things like this under wraps all the time; the freedom of the press and their right to publish anything of public interest was essential to the continued freedom of democracy. And if that also happened to improve his career, then all the better!

He knew that Amy probably wasn't going to open the door if she saw his car driving up, so he'd planned ahead and parked in a side street just outside of the estate and walked in through a little shortcut he knew that led to the back of her building. The fact that he was sneaking up on her flat by foot made him feel slightly guilty but he'd long ago learnt that feelings and morals could be something of an inconvenience to his profession if you didn't keep them in check. The trick was that you just had to be confident that you were doing the right thing for the greater good and that there was no good greater than the truth. Once you convinced yourself of that, there wasn't much you wouldn't do to get a story.

He approached Amy's flats from the rear and was just coming round the corner when he heard the front door of the building open. Not wanting to attract any undue attention, he ducked back behind the building and put his back flat against the wall, staying close enough to the edge so that he could peer around and still not be seen. He watched in surprise as he saw Amy exit the building followed by some guy that he'd never seen before. They were laughing and smiling! They weren't...? No, surely not, the guy looked like a geek with a fashion problem. Amy would never...

He watched them walk over to one of the cars parked in a visitor's bay. The bloke opened the car's boot and placed the picnic cooler he was carrying and Amy's shoulder bag in to it. He then opened the passenger door for her and she slipped in before he got into the driver's seat and drove them off. Kevin had already whipped out his mobile phone and quickly tapped the license plate number into it as they started to leave, before dashing back toward his own car.

It had taken him almost five minutes to walk from it to the flats but he managed to run the same distance in just under a minute and get into the vehicle just in time to see them drive past the road he'd parked in. He'd already started the engine and drove off before he'd put his seatbelt on. He was determined to follow them from a safe distance and see where they were going. He needed to find out who this guy was and what he was doing with Amy. She was always so trusting and with that nutter running around, well, God knows what could happen. Besides, he still needed to get his story on Mad Jack!

Mike had just driven out of the town centre when he looked in the mirror again to check what he suspected. "I don't mean to be paranoid but I think we're being followed," he said without looking away.

"What?" Amy glanced quickly behind then looked back sharply. "Oh my God."

"What's wrong?"

"It's my ex-boyfriend. The son of a bitch."

Mike tensed up. "Has he been stalking you?"

Amy shook her head. "Oh, no. Don't worry, he's not obsessive or anything like that and he certainly isn't dangerous; in fact, he's a complete wuss. I don't even think he wants me back. The problem is he's a reporter for the local rag and he thinks he can get information on the Mad Jack investigation out of me."

"Ah," Mike said. He was relieved and concerned at the same time. "I hope you don't mind me saying this but I really don't like reporters much."

"Something else we have in common. Let's pull over and have it out with him."

"Uh, we could do that, or we could just lose him."

Amy looked over at him and raised her eyebrows. "No offence intended, but are you that good a driver?" She'd found him to be a competent and safe chauffeur, but she was worried about what would happen if he attempted any sort of American cop show impersonation and started speeding along the A66.

Mike smiled. "Well, I wasn't planning to outrun him."

Amy found herself smiling too. "So what did you have in mind?" she asked with a slight giggle.

Kev continued to trail a short distance behind them. He was so proud of himself; they didn't have a clue that he was there. He hadn't considered exactly what he was going to do when they got to wherever they were heading but he'd figure something out. He always did in these circumstances.

Suddenly their car started to indicate left and exit the main road. Kev expertly let a couple of cars get between them and himself before taking the same exit and watched as they took one of the side roads that led to the entrance of a large supermarket. So that was it; they must have been going shopping. Why would she be doing her weekly shop with a loser like him? Sure enough, they turned into the first of the three large car parks of the store.

Kev, again, allowed another couple of vehicles to enter before following them in. He turned round the corner and expected to see them pulling into one of the parking spaces, but he didn't. In fact, he couldn't see them at all. He drove up and down all the lanes of spaces but couldn't see anything even resembling their car. Damn it, where had they gone? Maybe they'd driven through here and gone round into one of the other car parks.

Amy watched through the now tinted windows as Kev's car went up and down what must have been every lane before finally driving round to the next car park. She bit her lower lip and looked over at Mike; his eyes had glazed over so that they looked like they were completely solid black pearls. He'd told her before that this was what was called a trance state that mages entered when spell-casting. As soon as they'd turned into the car park, he'd pulled into the nearest space and cast the spell by twirling his index fingers in the air. Almost immediately, a shadow had seemed to descend over the car.

Once he was sure that Kev was safely out of sight, Mike stopped twirling his fingers and released the spell. The shadow veil lifted itself from around the car and his eyes returned to their normal light blue colour. He looked over at Amy and was pleased to see that she was grinning from ear to ear, clearly impressed. He gave her a grin of his own. "That was a veil."

"And it made us invisible?"

"Not quite. It alters people's perceptions of what's actually there. So, although your ex could see us, he didn't realise it was us or our car."

"Can most wizards do that?"

"Hmm, probably. It's quite a basic spell in principle, but it's one of those spells that's effectiveness is dependent on your own skill level. Basically, the more skilled you are at veils, the more impenetrable you can make it, as well as more difficult to detect. But even your basic wizard or witch can usually summon one that will block most unaided forms of perception. In fact, actually, now you mention it, it's one of the first spells most apprentices learn to help them keep the code."

Mike pulled out of the parking space and drove out of the car park the same way that they'd come in. Meanwhile, Amy reached into her tracksuit, removed a small notepad and started scribbling into it. Now she knew how Mad Jack may be avoiding the police.

Chapter 26

Roseberry Topping was located on the border between the county of North Yorkshire and the borough of Redcar and Cleveland. Mike had always liked to think of the Topping as being Middlesbrough's own little part of the beauty of Yorkshire. Although it was hardly the Moors or the Lake District, it was surrounded by plenty of woodland and moorland to keep most local walkers reasonably happy and, if nothing else, it was a nice place for parents to take their kids for some fresh air in the summer.

The summit of the hill itself had a distinctive half-cone shape, which Mike had once been told looked very similar to the Matterhorn in Switzerland. He'd always thought comparing the two was probably a bit unfair as he couldn't imagine the Topping ever achieving the same international tourist attraction status as its Swiss counterpart and Roseberry's height of just over a thousand feet hardly made it a candidate for mountaineering. In fact, most local kids had climbed it at least once before they were five!

Even Mike's own parents used to bring him to the Topping when he was young. They all used to go there for picnics and walks up the hill and then they'd go into the nearby village of Great Ayton and get an ice cream from Suggitts – the best sweet shop in the area. The top of Roseberry Topping also held a special place in Mike's heart for another reason as it was up there on one particularly quiet day that his father taught him his first spell. The old man showed him how to levitate some of the loose pebbles and stones. The top of Roseberry was where it all started. And where it all finished; something Mike tried his best to forget in order to avoid tarnishing all the good times.

Mike tried hard to push all the memories to the back of his mind as he drove into the visitors' area. He didn't want to be distracted while he was there with Amy. Despite remaining a popular place for locals to take their families for picnics at weekends during the summer months, the visitor car parks tended to be a lot quieter on weekdays, as well as weekends during the off-season. Mike's car was one of only three in the car park when they arrived. Despite this, the weather wasn't actually too bad for the time of year. Despite the fact that they'd had that heavy rain earlier in the week, the sky was now relatively clear and although there was a cool wind blowing, both Mike and Amy had worn coats which more than kept the chill out enough to make the day bearable.

As they emptied the car boot of their bags and the picnic lunch, Amy was more than a little surprised, and even a little nervous, when he also brought out a small cage that seemed to contain two mounds of white fur in it. "What are they?" she asked.

He looked at her awkwardly. "Uh, rats."

"Why have you...? No, wait, something tells me I don't want to know. At least not yet."

Mike smiled as he led her off the main walking route that went up the hill and instead took them all the way round to the opposite side, away from the car park. Eventually, the route opened up into a large open area with the Topping overshadowing it. He told her that this was where most local white witches came to practise their craft. Amy wasn't sure whether he was making fun of her or not. Still, she wasn't interested in that; it was wizardry she wanted to learn about so she could stop Mad Jack. "So," she asked as she placed the small picnic cooler she was carrying on the ground, "what are you going to show me now?"

Mike watched the mild wind blow her curly brown hair across her pretty face as he dropped the backpack he'd been carrying to the ground and carefully placed the cage down next to it. He was starting to wonder if he could concentrate enough for what he had planned. "Well. I've been thinking about what sort of spells Mad Jack's likely to be using to stop people finding him..."

"Yeah, that reminds me. There's something I want to ask you. You said that the Orders have authorities who ensure that the Code of Magic is enforced, right?" Mike nodded uncomfortably; he was dreading this question. "So how come they haven't stopped Mad Jack?"

He squirmed. "Uh, yeah, well, like I said, the Orders are responsible for keeping the Code." Amy stared at him. "And, um," he nervously continued, "they don't believe that one of their own can be responsible for such a thing."

"Say what?" she screamed.

He looked down nervously and tried to avoid eye contact. Damn it, please don't let them ruin this. "I'm sorry, the problem is that most wizards think that they're special. You see, they think that because they know things that most other people don't, that they are the only ones who see the world as it really is and therefore anyone who doesn't understand magic is a fool and unworthy of their concern. So they think that it's impossible for another of their kind…"

"Their kind?"

"Their words, not mine. They don't believe one of their own could be a killer."

Her face twisted and she gave him a harsh stare. "You mean the arrogant bastards think that it's not their problem because they think it couldn't possibly be one of them? How dare they…?" Her voice trailed off. Mike was afraid of this; he could tell she was angry and, if he was being honest, he didn't blame her. "They have no right, I mean, who's keeping an eye on them?"

Mike took another deep breath and paused for a moment, debating internally about whether he should tell her about the knights but decided that was too big a risk for both of them at this stage, so decided instead to say, "We are!"

He tried to swallow a gulp as he waited for her to respond. Amazingly, after taking another deep breath, her face softened somewhat and she even smiled slightly. "You're right," she said simply. Mike thought that was weird but decided to just file it away for later. "I'm sorry. You're right, it's not your fault. I think I'm starting to understand why you left the Order. Okay, so what exactly are you going to show me now?"

"Well," he said, secretly glad that she hadn't asked him whether there were any other authorities who could stop Mad Jack, "like I said, I was trying to think about what sort of spells he may have been using to avoid the police. I mean, we know that he's not using magic to kill his victims, but he must be using it to hide himself and then I got to thinking about what nearly happened to you the other night." Amy shuddered.

"And I realised that, like I said, he's probably been using enthralment to subdue all his victims. So I thought maybe if I showed you how that works, it might help us figure out his mantra."

"His what?"

"His mantra."

Amy made a face. "No offence intended, but I don't see how knowing what he chants for good luck is going to help me build a profile."

Mike laughed. "Oh, no, that's not what I meant. I'm talking about how he casts spells. You see, everyone casts spells differently. Some say incantations in ancient languages, others make gestures with their hands, like me, and some can even call upon their power through sheer force of will. The way that an individual casts their spells is what's known as their mantra. Now, if we can work out how he casts his spells, we'll learn a lot about him."

Her eyes suddenly lit up. "I get it, because the way in which he casts his spells is unique to him."

"Exactly. It'll also give us a good indication of his power."

"Okay." Suddenly she paused and looked at him suspiciously. "Wait a minute." She started to back away. "How are you going to demonstrate enthralment?"

"Oh, uh, not with you," he tried to reassure her. "Anyway, you are still wearing your crucifix, aren't you?" She reached toward her chest and nodded. "Good. Don't ever take it off and always keep your faith in it and you'll certainly be safe from magic. Not that you could probably be enthralled anyway."

"What do you mean?"

"Well, enthralment only works on those who are weak-willed, particularly if you know about it and, if I may say, you're one of the strongest willed people I've met."

This made her smile and blush slightly. "Thank you, that's..." She paused for a moment. "Nice to hear. So how exactly are you going to show me how enthralment works?"

Mike made a strange, nervous face and picked up the small cage with its furry white contents. Amy peered into the cage and observed the two animals laying in their confined prison. Their eyes were closed and their little bodies were pulsing lightly. Suddenly, she realised that they were sleeping peacefully despite being obviously confined.

"You've already enthralled them."

Mike nodded. "And let me tell you, it wasn't easy. I don't often use this type of spell, it really isn't my style of magic at all. Now watch this." He snapped his fingers and the rats suddenly opened their eyes and sprang to their feet. He then turned his index finger in a circular motion and the rats ran around the small cage in a circle. When he stopped rotating his finger, the rats stood still. He then made a sharp gesture with his hand upwards and they stood upright on their hind legs. He then made a sweeping motion and they came back down on all fours.

Amy was slightly disturbed by this little display but tried very hard not to let it show. "If I hadn't been wearing this," she said, holding her hand to her chest, "he'd have been able to do that to me."

Mike shook his head. "No, not exactly. I mean, these poor animals are just creatures of instinct. They're very easy to control and manipulate. People, who can think for themselves and have personalities, can't simply be turned into puppets like these things; it would take too much energy and effort. But I think he can probably enthral his victims to make them compliant enough to follow him without any conflict. And, like I said, I'm certain you'd be strong enough to stop someone from enthralling you."

Amy nodded thoughtfully. "So what you're saying is he can't make people do whatever he wants but you think he's powerful enough to make people who don't know about magic follow him back to his lair, so to speak?"

Mike made an odd gesture, half nodding and half shaking his head. "Sort of. I mean, this is one thing that's been really bothering me."

"What do you mean?"

"Well, like I say, enthralment doesn't give you complete control over someone; it merely makes them more compliant to your will. If you completely distrust someone, you won't go with them; your survival instincts are just too strong for that. It doesn't make sense."

Amy's eyes lit up and she dug out her notepad. "So maybe that's a reflection on his personality? You know, maybe he's someone people feel comfortable with?"

"Hmm, possibly. I mean there are ways he can increase his chances of making his enthralment work. If he has some part of the person – blood, hair or even just a personal possession – he'll have a greater spiritual link to the individual or he even just needs to know their name."

She gave him another shocked expression. "Seriously? That's true? Your name can be used against you?"

"Absolutely, but it's not a simple matter of knowing someone's name and you can have complete power over them. It's just another thing that you can use to increase your spell's potency. You see, what a lot of people don't realise is that words and names have power."

"What sort of power?"

"Hmm, maybe I should explain a few basic principles." He made another gesture with his hand and the rats laid back down asleep. He then placed the cage down and continued. "You see, like I told you the other day, magic is the study of the powers of the universe, the powers of this world, the next world and the individual. Now these powers aren't static, they can be transferred from one thing to another but not just into physical, tangible objects, but also to words and symbols. I mean, as you saw the other day, the circle and the star are intrinsically magical and are used in most aspects of symbology. Now the power of the soul that I just showed you can also be transferred; in fact, it's natural that it is."

"Natural? How?"

He smiled. "Well, you see there are three aspects that make up life: the mind, the body and the soul. The mind is who you are and your body is your vessel on this physical plane. Your soul is the energy that binds the two together. Now, as your body ages, your soul also depletes as it is transferred to other things, like people you love and things that are important to you, until, eventually, it fades and severs your mind's connection to this world. Your name is one of these things that your soul is transferred to because it's unique to you. Now, your soul is as unique to you as your DNA; in fact, even more so and even when it's been transferred to something else, it's still connected to you and so it provides what I can only describe as a sort of spiritual connection to you. So your name can be used as a sort of vessel to transmit power to or from you and also amplify it."

Amy stood there, scribbling odd notes, as he said all this and tried to take it all in. This was pretty heavy stuff and she knew she'd need to have a serious sit-down by herself to consider the implications of it all later, but for now she needed to concentrate and get the information she needed for the profile. The best way to do that was to carry on with her information gathering and keep asking questions. "Okay, so how does he cast his enthralment spell?" she asked.

Mike whistled through his teeth. "That's a tough one. Let's go through what we do know. He had a staff, so he's probably a wizard with the Order of the Cunning Ones and, judging from what he was saying when he blasted me with that fireball, I think it's safe to say that he uses incantations to call upon his power. That probably means he's not very powerful by the Order's standards."

"So incantation is the lowest form of spell-casting?"

"Generally. It's certainly the way the Order sees it. You start off as a 'wizard of incantation', then you become a 'wizard of gesture' and then the pinnacle is classed as a 'wizard of will'." It was at this point that he noticed that she was scribbling in her notepad at a frantic pace. "Uh, am I going too fast for you?"

"Oh, not at all," she said as she continued to scribble. "I think I've more or less got it now."

* * *

A couple of hours later, they were sitting on a picnic blanket on the other side of the hill, munching on the sandwiches Amy had made for them. Well, they were a bit more elaborate than simple sandwiches. She had made each of them a baguette with chicken, cheese, salad and mayonnaise. Mike found it difficult to eat the baguette as he wasn't too good with crusty bread, so he ate it as slowly as possible to try and avoid making too much of a mess. His mum always complained that she thought he ate way too quickly anyway. He supposed that she'd be really chuffed to see him eating so slowly now.

He turned and looked at his dining companion. Despite her small size and tiny mouth, she was succeeding in eating her baguette without any mess and with complete elegance. How did she do it? She noticed him looking and gave him a sweet smile. He smiled back sheepishly like a kid caught looking at an expensive toy his parents couldn't afford for Christmas.

"So," she asked as she finished her latest mouthful, "how is the Order structured exactly?"

Mike shrugged. "Well, there's sort of an informal hierarchy. The Order of the Cunning Ones is huge; it's the largest Order in Britain, you know, and Europe, for that matter. But it also has Chapters in most places around the world."

"Chapters?"

"Sorry, I'm getting ahead of myself. Basically, the Order's divided up into local Chapters which are virtually autonomous entities in their own right. They're a bit like gentlemen's social clubs where wizards can get together and meet up to discuss magic and practise spells. The head of a local Chapter is called a vice-mage;

there's also a head of the entire Order, who's called the arch-mage."

"So basically wizards practise magic as a hobby?"

Mike hummed. "Some do, but the Order has a lot of wizards on staff as well. There are basically two main occupations for wizards. Keepers are the cops, effectively. They enforce the Code of Magic. Then there are seekers, like I used to be, who research magic and try to find new spells and ways of performing them. There's also support staff of course, like alchemists, who make gold and diamonds to fund the Order."

"You're kidding me!"

"How else do you think they make their money? There's also other staff who have more mundane tasks, in fact, that bloke you saw the other day is the Teesside Chapter's treasurer."

"Teesside has its own Chapter? How many wizards are there round here?"

"Oh most counties in the UK have at least one Chapter. Teesside's pretty small. I think there are only about two hundred members, including the local keepers."

"Incredible." Mike had seen the look that was now showing on her face before; finding that there was a whole other world that you'd never realised was right under your nose was an awful lot to take in. Maybe it was time to change the subject.

"So you think you've got enough to build a profile now?" he asked between bites of the delicious sandwich.

"I think I can certainly get a preliminary profile on him produced now," she replied without a hint of any chewing being interrupted. "Would you like to see it when I'm done?"

He smiled warmly. "I'd like that," was his reply and it was one of the truest statements he'd ever made.

She returned the smile. "By the way, where did you get those things from?" she asked, pointing at the caged rats.

"Oh, believe it or not, from the pet shop downtown."

"What? They sell those things as pets?"

"Apparently. According to the guy who sold me them, white rats are specifically bred for pets."

"Are you serious?"

"I'm afraid so."

Amy shook her head, "So what are you going to do with them?"

"I've no idea." He laughed and she laughed too. "Maybe I'll keep them. I need some company." It was only as he said this that he realised what he was saying! He worried what she would say next but she smiled at him knowingly.

"Oh, don't say that. You're not completely alone, are you?"

"No, of course not. I have friends and good colleagues and family," he found himself saying.

"But I bet your house gets lonely sometimes?" she asked.

"Yeah, I guess so," he replied.

"So what was it like?" she then asked, suddenly changing the subject.

"What?" he asked.

"Being a wizard."

"Hmm, it was fun, I suppose. I mean, I got to do all sorts of stuff that was interesting, but the world that they live in is very confining and very dangerous."

"So's this one."

He nodded solemnly. "True."

She paused. "Sorry, I keep forgetting you knew the last victim. Kerry, wasn't it?"

He nodded again. "Yeah. She was a good kid."

"How well did you know her?"

"Not very well. I only saw her once a week, if that, but she seemed like a good student with a lot of potential. Full of life, full of energy." He sighed.

Amy looked at him closely and intently, directly into his eyes. Mike thought for a minute that she was trying to look into his very soul. Then, slowly, she reached out and took his hand in her own. It felt like soft satin. "We'll get him," she promised. He smiled and nodded, trying hard not to forget what had brought them together and what they were trying to do. They sat there for a moment before Amy said, "I really think we should get back so I can finish the profile."

He nodded. "Yeah, okay." With that, they finished the last of the sandwiches and headed back home.

Chapter 27

Middlesbrough's Transporter Bridge was the largest working bridge of its kind in the world. Spanning 850 feet across the River Tees, standing 225 feet high and made by the famous Dorman Long company, Frank never failed to be impressed whenever he came down to do his structural inspection. He wasn't expected to meet the others there until nine but he always liked to get there for eight and stand in the magnificence of this marvellous piece of engineering for an hour and soak up the history and atmosphere of it.

He'd parked near the base of the south towers and planned to just stand around for an hour or so and enjoy the fresh air. He noticed the dark blue duffel bag as soon as he got out of the car. *Damn it*, he thought, *kids today have no respect for history, dumping their rubbish on a great monument to engineering like this.* Well, he wasn't going to have anything spoil today's inspection and he had plenty of time to drive out to the dump and get rid of the bag before the others arrived.

He strode over to the offending object, bent down, grabbed it and froze. He released his grip and looked at his hand; it was covered in something wet, sticky and red!

Mike scribbled over the equation and rewrote it again in his notebook for what must have been the fourteenth time in as many minutes. He was really wishing he could use his shadow writing but that wasn't a luxury he could risk at the university, even in the privacy of his own office.

After he'd dropped Amy off at her flat on Saturday evening, he'd joined a couple of friends for a quick pint and a game of pool before heading home to get some much needed rest. He thought that the next day was going to crawl by but he slept most of the morning and was up just in time to get over to his mum's for Sunday dinner.

He was quite proud of himself that he'd managed to avoid going in to too much detail about what he'd been up to the previous week, but he was sure that she knew something was up. He just hoped that she'd put it down to Kerry's death, but a part of him knew that was extremely unlikely. His mother didn't need to be psychic or know any magic to figure him out, she had enough insight as it was to tell when people were lying or keeping things from her. Especially her own son! Still, he couldn't worry too much about that now.

He'd had no lectures or tutorials on Monday morning so he was planning to make use of the time to catch up with some of his research projects, but he just couldn't concentrate. Part of him was still thinking about everything that had happened the last week and another part of him was wondering what was going to happen when Amy completed her profile.

First there was the problem of how they were going to use it to point the police in the right direction of Mad Jack and do it in a way that meant nobody would get hurt. But there was also another thing that was nagging away at him and that was what was going to happen after they'd actually caught him? Specifically, Mike wondered, what was going to happen between Amy and him. Would she still want to know him after all this was done? He also felt guilty about even thinking about it; after all, there were bigger things to worry about, like Kerry. He stared down at the equation with such intent that he started to wonder if he was trying to will the numbers to tell him something.

Just then, he heard someone tapping on his open door. He was half-expecting a student with a question about something but instead saw the smiling face of Dr Ranjit Patel from the computer science department. "Hiya, mate," he said cheerfully, "do you fancy going for lunch?"

Mike looked up at the clock and saw that it was nearly lunchtime. Maybe a bite to eat would help him concentrate. "Yeah, sure, why not?" he said and grabbed his jacket.

Dave pushed his way through the crowd of screaming vultures and ducked underneath the police tape that now barricaded the south towers of the transporter bridge off from the rest of the world. He stared over at the crime scene, watching Jenny flit back and forth between the pathologist and the SOCOs, trying to get a picture of what the hell had happened.

Dave decided to stay well out of it for a moment to try and calm himself down. He knew exactly what had happened; the bastard had done it again right under their bloody noses. Dave looked up at the sky and closed his eyes, the cold air was stinging his cheeks like a thousand needles but he just didn't care. Outwardly, he was trying to project an air of calm indifference but inside he was trying to contain a sense of boiling rage. He was damned if he was going to let this continue; this madman was going to be stopped and be it through hell or high water, he was going to be the one who did it.

He lowered his head and began striding toward the small group of SOCOs knelt down near the base of the tower. Jenny noticed his approach and began bounding over to him with her long open coat flapping around her like a large grey cloak.

"Sir," she said as she stopped briefly in front of him then broke out into a stride beside him, matching him step for step.

"Sergeant, just give it to me straight." The cold wind continued to flap her coat round her as she laid out the grizzly details for him. There was no question; same MO, same guy, he'd done it again. "Who found the body?" Dave asked as he pulled on a pair of disposable plastic gloves, identical to the pair Jenny was wearing, making an almost painful snapping sound in the process.

"A site inspector. Apparently, there was an inspection scheduled on the bridge this morning and he liked to come down early. He saw the duffel bag and thought it had been dumped so he went over to move it and got a handful of the victim's blood."

Dave shook his head. Poor sod; he wasn't going to forget that any time soon. They'd now reached the small group of SOCOs in their gleaming white disposable overalls, who all shuffled to one side or the other so that Dave could get a better look at what they were guarding. Dr Sam Edmonds, the grumpy old coroner, was knelt by a large blue duffel bag, identical to six others that Dave had seen before. The bag had been completely unzipped to reveal its grizzly contents.

Dave stopped dead in his tracks and hoped nobody saw him swallow uncomfortably. This one was different. This one was worse, much worse. Even though she'd been stabbed and mutilated like the others, her wounds were deeper and more violent, more severe. She'd fought back, she'd suffered. From the look and the smell of her, it also seemed that she'd been here a while.

"All right, so what have we got, Sam?" Dave finally found the courage to ask.

The old man sighed. "What have we got? What have we got? What we've got is a monster, a fucking monster, that's what! Do you see what he's bloody done to her? Before you ask, yes, she's probably been sexually assaulted and, yes, it is different from the others. There's definite signs of a struggle, she's got a lot of defensive wounds and it seems that…" He paused. "That she may have been choking on something, like something was shoved in her mouth and, no, he wasn't stupid enough to leave it there."

"How long's she been here?"

"At least a couple of days. I won't know for certain until I get her back to the lab."

Dave closed his eyes again briefly then stood up and looked back at Jenny. "Do we have an ID on her?"

Jenny nodded. "Yeah, like all the others, her wallet was left in the bag with her."

Dave waited patiently. "And?"

Jenny pulled her coat closed round herself to keep out the cold and sighed. "Well, you're not gonna believe this…"

Mike had left the university doors with Ranjit dead on the clocks turning 12. Though the department had a very liberal view on timekeeping, like most academic institutions, there was something in Mike's character that meant he'd always been nervous about taking an extended lunch break, or even starting lunch any time before midday. He usually went to Greggs for a sandwich but decided that he'd earned a little treat and instead opted for a mince and onion pie. Normally, he went back to his office to eat, but he again felt like he deserved a change and continued with Ranjit into the town centre, where they sat down on one of the benches between the two main shopping centres.

"So, what were you up to on Saturday?" Ranjit asked.

Mike gave him what he hoped was a coy smile and, through a bite of his pie, said, "Wouldn't you like to know."

"Come on, man. You're never this coy." When Mike remained silent, he said, "Who is she? Val told me she saw you with some girl last week."

"Ah, so I'm the subject of office gossip."

"Oh, come on, man, Krisha wants to know the details so we can invite you both round for dinner."

"Look, Ranj, I appreciate the thought, but—" He was almost finished with the pie when his mobile phone rang, interrupting him. "Sorry, mate. Hold on." He shoved the last of the mince-filled pastry into his mouth and fumbled in his pocket before flipping his phone out. "Hello, Dr Walker speaking."

"Yes, hello, Dr Walker, this is Detective Sergeant Granger."

Granger. He shuffled through the cobwebs of his memory then remembered her as the female CID officer who interviewed him the other week about Kerry's death. God, poor Kerry; in all the haste of the last week he'd nearly all but forgotten. Wait, maybe they'd caught the bastard? "Oh yeah, hello, Sergeant. Has there been any progress?"

"Um, yes, sir, that's why I'm calling. There's been a development and we were wondering if you would mind coming down the station again, please?"

"Yeah, of course. I can come right now, if you like. Okay, will do." He turned off his phone and turned to Ranjit. "Sorry, mate, I've got to go." His friend was about to speak but Mike cut him off. "And, before you ask, no that wasn't her. It's the police about Kerry; they've got something to tell me." He stood up.

"Ah, so she does exist!"

Mike sighed. "I'll tell you about her later."

"Okay, mate," Ranjit said with a smile, then looked serious. "You all right going on your own?"

"I'll be fine," he said and waved his friend goodbye, saying he'd catch up with him later.

Mike was a bit surprised that the police wanted to see him again and he was even more shocked that the sergeant was insistent that he came down to the station as soon as possible. Still, he couldn't think of any other reason than that they'd found some sort of evidence that they needed his help with. Possibly they wanted to go over something in his statement. Maybe he could help them stop Mad Jack now, or maybe even find something that would help Amy's profile and tell her, and... Damn, he was getting ahead of himself and, besides, he had to remember what this was all about. People were dying, for God's sake!

Sergeant Granger was waiting for him by the lift door. "Good afternoon, Sergeant. What is it that can't wait?"

The young woman was silent for a second, then said, "If you could just come with me, please, sir."

Her voice was flat and obviously meant to be emotionless, but Mike was sure he could detect a slight nervousness in it, even without using his psychic power. He suddenly felt slightly worried as he followed her into the lift. It didn't escape his notice that they were going down instead of up. A knot was developing in his stomach. When they reached the basement floor, she gestured him out first before following behind. A part of him knew that he should be asking where they were going but a larger part of him already knew the answer. As he walked through the large, double doors to the morgue, he recognised the inspector he'd met at his previous visit, standing by a cloth-covered table.

"Hello, sir," the inspector said as he approached. "Tell me, do you recognise this girl?"

Before Mike could say anything, the inspector pulled the cloth away to reveal the naked, battered, bruised, mutilated, and already decomposing body of a young blonde female. Even though it was cut to ribbons and turning a rather unsightly shade of green, Mike could still recognise the clear, unique outlines of Tracy's face.

His legs nearly turned to jelly and the pie he'd just eaten decided that it didn't want to be in his stomach anymore. He somehow managed to run over to the sink he'd seen in the room and threw up violently. Just as the last of the lunch he'd just consumed was regurgitated, the inspector walked over toward him, slowly and deliberately. As Mike looked up at the copper's face, he suddenly remembered what the man's name was and what Amy had said her brother's occupation was!

Chapter 28

Amy leaned back in her chair and threw her arms up in satisfaction. "Yes!" she screamed out loud before hitting the print command.

She'd had to work all through Sunday and Monday, but she was now sure that she'd finally cracked the profile; or at least had it in a good enough format for a first draft to give Dave a preliminary report and start making enquiries. Finally, they were going to get somewhere and stop the bastard before he could hurt anybody else.

She picked up the print-out from her printer and hurried to get her coat. First thing was first, though; before she showed Dave, there was someone's opinion, and more importantly, approval, she had to get.

"Come on, Walker. What do you know? Are you seriously expecting us to believe that it's pure coincidence that the last two victims were both students of yours?"

Mike just sat in the interview room and stared ahead, looking at neither the inspector or Sergeant Granger, who was as silent as he was. He'd said nothing since seeing Tracy's lifeless body in the morgue, cut up like a piece of slowly rotting meat. He didn't respond when the sergeant had offered him a handkerchief after he'd lost his lunch. Nor did he respond in any way as the three of them took the lift up to the interview room and sat down, as the inspector asked him time and time again how it was possible that he had a link to both of the last two victims and it not be just a tragic coincidence.

He just couldn't respond; on a certain level he couldn't even hear their questions. Even before Kerry, he'd seen death. In many ways, you couldn't know about the Arts and not be touched by it. When he'd seen Kerry the other week, he'd remembered his own brush with death but it was almost as if he was detached from the memory as a bystander looking in from the outside. He'd remembered the pain and numbness he'd felt and realised Kerry's parents must have been feeling the exact same thing. It was one of the main reasons he'd decided to make it his business to stop the serial killer and prevent anyone else feeling that pain.

He'd failed.

Tracy was dead.

Now her parents were going to go through that pain and numbness.

He'd failed.

Just like he had before.

Inspector Walsh continued to demand an answer without getting one. As he thought of that name, another emotion started to creep into Mike's mind and body. He couldn't believe he'd been such a fool. Amy had used him to get what she needed to help her brother. She wasn't interested in him at all. He should have known. How could he have been so stupid? He finally turned his attention to Walsh. "Tell me, Inspector, am I under arrest?"

Now it was Walsh's turn to stare at Mike silently.

"No, sir. You're not," Sergeant Granger said calmly. Walsh turned around and stared at her sharply.

While he was distracted Mike stood up. "Then, if you don't mind, I've just seen two of my students brutally murdered in as many weeks so I'm not in any fit state to give a statement just now. Therefore, if you don't mind, I'd like to leave immediately."

When he walked round the table, Walsh stood up and blocked his path. "Now you sit—"

"Stop it, sir!" Walsh looked down at Sergeant Granger, astonished. She gave him a long stare. Her eyes were almost glazed over.

Even though he could only glance at her from the side, Mike could tell that she was pleading with the inspector. When he looked up at the policeman's face, Mike saw the detective's eyes close slowly. He then moved to one side and Mike walked out the door.

Jenny stood up slowly, without so much as a glance at the inspector. "It's over, sir. I'm sorry." She couldn't even look at him. Dave just stood there and heard the door close behind her as she left.

Amy found she had a slight spring in her step as she approached the university building. She really hoped Mike liked her profile and didn't think that it revealed too much about the magical world. She didn't want to do anything that would risk exposing him or placing him in danger. That would be terrible after everything he'd done for her. Besides, they needed to find a way to use the profile to find the guy. They couldn't exactly just say to Dave, 'Oh, by the way, you're looking for a wizard!' But they needed to do something. Maybe they could set up some sort of sting to find out who Mad

Jack was and then they could tell Dave where to find him. Maybe Mike would have an idea.

She wondered what would happen after they caught Mad Jack. Maybe Mike and her could keep in touch and possibly even get to know each other better. Well, that would depend on what the future would bring, she supposed, but still, it never hurt to help it along if you could.

She really liked Michael Walker; he was kind and sweet, not to mention kind of cute. Was he allowed to be with a non-magic user? He hadn't said that he couldn't be and that thought brought a smile to her face as she entered the foyer and walked up to the reception to ask if Mike was available. The receptionist, a middle-aged blonde woman whose name tag identified her as 'Valerie', apologised, saying that he'd left for lunch and had then later phoned to say that he would be out of the office for a while but hoped to return later in the afternoon.

Although disappointed, Amy handed the manila envelope she'd been carrying over to the receptionist and asked her to pass it on to Mike as soon as he got back. "Could you ask him if he could have a look at it and let me know what he thinks of it as soon as possible, please?" Valerie nodded with a reassuring smile, which Amy returned before leaving.

She swung the heavy door open so quickly that she heard the 'thud' before feeling the impact. She looked round and was horrified to see the small man Mike had told her was the Treasurer of the Order of The Cunning Ones, clutching his nose. "Oh dear. I'm so sorry," she blurted out as the man regained his feet and smiled at her nervously.

"Oh, that's quite all right, my dear, no damage done." He looked at her in a very confused and nervous manner as he adjusted his tie.

Amy smiled warmly. "Sorry, you're trying to think where you've seen me before. I was meeting Mike when you came to see him the other day."

He seemed to relax and smiled before extending his hand. "Oh yes, of course, miss. I'm sorry, uh, my name's Simpkins, uh, Peter Simpkins."

"Amy Walsh," She replied as she shook his hand. "Uh, if you're going to see Mike, then I wouldn't bother, the receptionist has just told me that he's out this afternoon."

"Oh dear, that's a shame. I'll have to catch him later. Thank you for letting me know."

"Oh, so you were going to see him?"

"Oh, yes. Uh, my employer wanted me to ask him some questions about some work he did for us."

Amy raised her eyebrows. "Really. What did Mike do for your employer?"

Simpkins gulped. "Uh, research."

Amy looked at him sceptically. "I thought he'd left—" She covered her mouth with her hand as quickly as she could when she realised what she was saying.

Simpkins looked slightly shocked. "Uh, do you know what sort of research he used to do for us?"

Amy decided to be coy. "Maybe." She started to walk off. Simpkins stared after her for a moment then suddenly jogged up and broke into a stride beside her. Amy was a bit unnerved. "Can I help you with something?"

"Uh, forgive me." He'd dropped his voice. "But are you helping Dr Walker find him?" She looked at him, slightly shocked. "It's just that the vice-mage has asked me to help Michael track him down."

She stopped dead in her tracks and stared at him. "Sorry?" Why hadn't Mike told her that? Then she remembered some of the things he'd said and also some of the things he hadn't said. Like exactly why he'd left the Order. Her instincts told her that it wasn't on good terms.

"I was just wondering if maybe I could be of any assistance to you both?" Amy was suspicious. Mike didn't exactly seem friends with this guy from what she saw the other day and she'd got the impression that he wasn't on best of terms with the Order.

"Thank you, Mr Simpkins, but no thank you."

"Um, are you sure? Has Dr Walker ever shown you our Order?"

She looked at him critically. "No," was her calm reply, having now noticed something over the street that worried her.

"Would you like to see it? Perhaps I could introduce you to the vice-mage?"

"No thank you, Mr Simpkins. Now, if you don't mind, I must be on my way."

The little man looked crestfallen, but said, "Of course, miss, I'm sorry." He then scurried off in the opposite direction. Amy waited until he was out of sight before heading off herself, now more eager than ever to speak to Mike.

Kev was just walking back toward the university building when he saw the two of them and quickly dashed across the street, trying to keep out of sight. Things were getting more and more interesting.

He'd been secretly trailing Michael Walker all day after he'd found out from a 'friend' in the DVLA that that was who he'd seen picking up Amy the previous day. He was more than a little surprised to find that he was a physics lecturer at the university. What on Earth could Amy be doing with him? Well, he was determined to find out, so he made a point of watching Walker that morning to try and find out exactly what he was working on for her.

Obviously, all this was something to do with the Mad Jack case; there was no other logical explanation. He knew that the last victim had been a physics student at the university so obviously this Walker had something to do with the investigation. His suspicions were confirmed when the scientist got that call at lunchtime when he was out with his crony and left him to go to the police station. Damn, what Kev would have given to know what was going on in there.

Realising that he couldn't get anything more from hanging around the cop shop, he decided to head back to the university and wait for Walker to show up. He was just approaching the entrance when he saw Amy and some older guy of short stature with a balding head walking away from it. Thinking that the old guy had glanced over at him, Kev thought quickly and stayed on the other side of the road so he could observe them while pretending to check something on his smartphone. However, they soon parted ways and Kev found himself with a choice of which one to follow, but decided that he should stick with Amy.

He crossed over the road and turned the corner only to almost run straight into her, standing there with her hands on her hips!

Chapter 29

Mike walked slowly back toward the university as if he was in a trance. He later wondered if people thought they were seeing a zombie on the streets of Middlesbrough.

He couldn't believe what had just happened. It was safe to assume that this could definitely be added to the list of worst days of his life. So far, the only semi-good thing had been that at least, this time, there had been no reporters waiting for him outside the police station. The anger had subsided somewhat, at least for now. He just felt numb and not just because of Tracy's death; he felt used and violated. He knew Amy Walsh wanted to know about magic so that she could build up her profile to stop Mad Jack, but he hadn't thought that she was only doing it for her brother. Now he'd met him and seen what he was like. Was she just doing it for him and using Mike to get what he needed? He wouldn't be at all surprised; it was the story of his life. The anger was creeping back in as he walked past the reception and Val called him over.

He sighed and walked over to her. "Yeah, Val, what is it?"

"Oh, yes, Mike. Your lady friend, miss, uh, I mean Dr Walsh dropped this off for you."

He took the envelope from her and nodded solemnly. "Thanks, Val. Is she still around?"

"No, actually I think I saw her go with that nice Mr Simpkins who came to visit you last week. She bumped into him as she was leaving. I think she must have told him you were out."

Great, she was probably going to try and wheedle some information out of him now. Well, let her. Simpkins could have the fun of answering her stupid questions. Let her use him for a change. Maybe he'd even take her to the Order; the poor little sod was probably desperate for some attention.

Something must have shown on Mike's face because Val suddenly asked him, "Uh, is everything okay, Mike?"

He thought he was going to lie but found himself shaking his head and saying, "No, Val. It isn't." He walked back upstairs to his office.

"Oh, hi, Amy," Kev said, doing his best attempt to feign surprise. "Fancy bumping into you. How—"

"Shut up and cut the crap, Kev. I'm warning you. You stay away from me and Mike."

"Mike?"

"Mike Walker. Who you very well know works here and you know I went out on a date with on Saturday, as you followed us!"

"Um, well, I..."

"Let me make two things clear. One – we're over and we're never getting back together. And, two – if you bother me or Mike again then I'll report you for stalking. Now piss off!" With that, she turned on her heels and stormed off.

Kev gulped as he took in what she'd just said. She was dating Michael Walker? That was it? There was no help with the Mad Jack investigation? He stood there for a moment, trying to gather his thoughts, before deciding that he needed to think about this more. He turned to head back to his office, only to feel a ping at the back of his neck, which made him stop for a second and turn around suddenly, but he saw nothing. He shrugged and was about to go back to the *Gazette*'s office but suddenly he stopped and turned around to head back towards Amy.

Chapter 30

Amy was almost back at the CPS when she felt a tap on the back of her shoulder and found Kev standing there. "I thought I told you—" she started.

"Amy, wait, please, I'm sorry."

"What?"

"I need to speak to you. It's important. It's about Mad Jack. I've found out something."

"You've what?"

"I found out something but I need your help."

"What are you talking about?" she asked, now very suspicious.

"I think I've found..." He paused for a moment like he was gathering his thoughts. "Where he is."

"Say what?" What the hell was he's saying?

"But it makes no sense." This got her attention. "It's like he can disappear!"

Amy froze at this and was silent for a moment. Had Kev really? She wasn't sure what to say but went for, "What are you talking about, Kev?"

He smiled and said, "Let me show you." He paused again, then said, "Please."

Under normal circumstances, she would have thought this was him trying to get her back but there was something about the way he spoke that made her think that this was different. What should she do? Damn it, she didn't like Kev anyway near as much as she used to but if he got in over his head and something happened to him... "Okay." She sighed. "Show me what you've found."

Mike walked into his office and threw the manila envelope onto his desk before picking up his bag. Whatever it was that she wanted, it could wait. Maybe Simpkins could help her out with it. He headed out the door and slammed it behind him. He needed to get home.

Kev led Amy round a corner to the back of a building that backed on to the *Gazette* office. "Kev, where are we going?" she asked as he stopped in front of a solid wall.

"Here," was all he said as he touched the wall. There was something about the sound of his voice that made her uneasy; he almost didn't sound like Kev. She was about to tell him that she was going to leave when the wall he had his hand on started to shimmer and she watched in awe as a small door appeared.

"Kev, how the hell did you—" A violent thud to the back of her head cut off her sentence and she remembered nothing more as the magic door slowly opened.

Chapter 31

Mike was halfway down the corridor when he stopped, sighed and turned back. Once he was back inside his office, he dropped his bag in the spare chair by the door and sat at his desk.

Begrudgingly, he picked up the manila envelope, stuck his little finger under the flap and ripped it open furiously, resulting in a paper cut. "Shit," he swore under his breath and sucked on the finger, wondering if maybe she'd cursed the bloody thing.

He shook his head at his own stupidity and pulled out the wad of paper. The front page was mostly blank with just a few words in the dead centre, in large print, which read *Preliminary Psychological Profile of Unidentified Subject 001 aka 'Mad Jack' by Dr Amy Walsh, BSc, PhD.* So that was it; she wanted him to check her stupid profile. He first entertained thoughts of just throwing it away, then he considered just ignoring it but, ultimately, his curiosity got the better of him and he started to read.

The subject is most likely to be a Caucasian male in his mid-thirties to early forties.

He will most likely be shorter than average height and perhaps slightly overweight and balding.

He will come from a family connected with a particular occupation that is a long tradition for them, most likely one that requires a high degree of intelligence and expertise, but one that the subject himself likely lacks real skill in. Thusly, he has had to settle for a more menial job, most likely an office role but still somewhat connected to his family's traditional occupation, such as a secretary at the family firm.

He will most likely come from a strict family and is probably the youngest of several siblings, all of which are skilled in the occupation that his family has traditionally followed. He will feel intense bitterness toward them for this but will not dare show it to them or anyone else in his family. He also most likely despises most of his co-workers but, again, does not display this outwardly.

His co-workers probably think he is capable in his role but look down on him somewhat due to his lack of prowess in their occupation. Despite this, he will not appear outwardly angry. In fact, for most of the time, when he is not committing his offences, he will appear almost shy, timid and unthreatening, possibly even the type of person most people feel safe and even comfortable around, the type of person people notice but don't notice, always there, always in the background. Therefore, as an individual, he will not seem all that unusual and will, for all intents and purposes, appear 'normal' most of the time. He can therefore be classed as a sociopath. He is also likely to have very few or, more likely, no friends. In short, a total loner.

He will mostly keep both his workspace and his home perfectly neat and tidy, possibly bordering on an obsessive scale.

He most likely started his crimes when he was angered by the first victim, who reminded him of someone who he feels wronged him in his 'normal' life, most likely a member of his family or a work colleague. Since he feels he lacks the strength, confidence or power to face people he hates in his day-to-day life, he lashes out at someone who reminds him of them and finds that he can successfully overpower them.

At least one or two more of his victims followed this pattern of reminding him of people he feels have wronged him. After he became confident in his technique, he then moved on to taking women who he is attracted to, as he has never felt confident enough to even approach them before but now feels not only confident but entitled to anything (and anyone) that he wants.

He will also be taking some sort of trophy from his victims, perhaps in the form of simply a few drops of blood to relive the experience later and continue to gloat his superiority over them.

Now that he is aware that he is being hunted by the police, he will probably monitor the case through the media and will most likely try to learn about the investigation itself if at all possible. However, he will not inject himself directly into the investigation by contacting the police but will try and find out any information he can from other people connected to it such as journalists who may be following the investigation or possibly even talking to a victim's family, offering sympathy.

As he will never be satisfied in his working life, he will never be satisfied in his private life without killing and will therefore continue to kill until he is apprehended.

Mike humphed under his breath and sighed as he threw the profile back on the desk. Well, that was just great.

That description could relate to any number of wizards. Well, maybe not Jon and certainly not Chris.

It sounded like Simpkins, though. He was short and chubby and lacked decent magical ability. And he had two brothers who were both powerful wizards and...

Mike sat up sharply.

Kevin Turner dragged the unconscious Amy through the magical door into the small, neat office.

And he was in his late thirties.

Simpkins looked down at the thin chain wrapped around her neck. With one swift action, he yanked the crucifix off her neck and threw it on his desk.

And he was working in a menial office job in the Order.

"Pick her up," Simpkins told Turner, as he held a piece of card with a single hair on it.

And he was always nervous.

Simpkins retrieved a small object from his desk drawer then picked up his staff and clicked his fingers.

And, he'd come to see Mike, asking about his own suspicions about the Mad Jack investigation.

But that was for Chris, wasn't it?

Mike gulped.

No it wasn't!

"Oh, bloody hell!"

Mike ran out the door so fast that he nearly broke the hinges clean off!

The three of them materialised in the Order's car park. Mad Jack told Kevin Turner to put Amy Walsh in the boot of his car then get in the passenger seat. He watched the reporter carry out his orders with a smirk, then looked down at the other piece of card he'd picked up that still had Amy Walsh's hair on it. He never threw anything away! He then got into the car and drove off with his prizes.

Chapter 32

Mike didn't know how he was now so sure, but he was certain Peter Simpkins was Mad Jack!

The bastard had killed seven people, including Kerry and Tracy!

God, he'd killed Kerry!

He'd killed Tracy! God, he'd killed Tracy!

And now Amy was with him!

How could he have missed it? It was all so obvious. That night when he'd saved Amy, the madman was more or less the same height as her, just like Simpkins! And he had the same type of simple wooden staff!

Mike had run round the corner to the Order even faster than he had when he'd produced the geographic profile. He had to stop once he reached the entrance to catch his breath. He was panting so heavily that he could barely breathe, but he knew he couldn't wait. Frantically he shuffled through his pockets, searching for the amulet. Shit, he couldn't find it. Don't say that this was the one day he'd forgotten to bring it with him. Finally, after what seemed like an eternity, he felt the thin silver chain around his fingers. He pulled it out of his pocket with shaking hands and threw it over his head without pausing for another moment, before slamming through the double doors into the building.

He stood in the entrance for a moment and opened his mind, looking for what he knew of Simpkins' aura, but it was no good; he just couldn't find it. By this time, the spectral butler had formed in front of him. Mike ran through him before he could ask what he wanted and then opened his mind again, this time looking for another, more familiar, aura.

He traversed the complex path of corridors that he'd followed twice before and once again found himself outside his old master's office. He banged on the door furiously and yelled for the vice-mage to answer. He was just about ready to try and break the seal again when suddenly the door swung open and Chris peered out with an intent look on his face.

"Oh, it's you. What is it now, Michael?"

Without thinking, Mike grabbed hold of the old man's robes and pulled him forward until they were face to face. "Where is he? Where's Simpkins' office?"

"What?"

"Simpkins, the treasurer. Where's his office? Please, God, Chris, in the name of everything that's holy, where's his office?"

The vice-mage must have been so shocked by the pleading entering Mike's voice that he found himself instinctively answering, "Uh, it's three doors down on the right. Why?" Mike released his grip and dashed along the corridor, with Chris calling behind him, "What's going on, Michael? Michael!"

But Mike didn't answer; he was already at the door the vice-mage had indicated and was placing his hand upon it. Mike had always had a natural talent for protective wards. When he was a seeker he'd created thousands and he knew the ins and outs of most of them by heart. Simpkins' ward was much cruder than the one on Chris' door and it took Mike less than a second to find the flaw in it. He could have delicately chipped it away, like unpicking a tapestry, so that the door would simply unlock but he had no time for that and he just blasted as much of his power as possible into the weak spot and the door literally exploded into the room in a mess of splintered wood.

He barged into the small room and looked around. The office was almost disturbingly neat. The single bookshelf had all the books arranged by both size and colour and all the papers on the desk were stacked neatly in completely straight, perfectly square stacks.

"What on earth is going on here, Michael?" Mike didn't even turn around to look at Chris standing in the doorway; he was too busy staring at Simpkins' desk. "Look at the mess you've made. The alchemists are going charge a fortune to repair this door!" He walked into the room and shook his head. "And look at that. Simpkins has left his back entrance visible."

Mike looked up sharply and noticed that there was a second door on the back wall – one of the magic doors wizards used to get in and out of the Order quietly without being seen.

"Oh my God!"

Mike grabbed the small object that he had been staring at off the desk and virtually smashed the magic door open. He found himself in the back street behind the Order. He looked up and down frantically but could see no one. His hands were gripped into such tight fists that Amy's crucifix almost dug completely into the palm of his right hand.

Chapter 33

Dave left the Super's office and closed the door behind him slowly and deliberately. Well that was it. He'd lost the case. It wasn't as bad as he'd expected. Shaw had simply said that it was time for a fresh pair of eyes and recommended Dave take a break as he'd been working too hard. Williams had been very pleasant and gracious, even shaking Dave's hand and saying what a great job he'd done on the investigation.

Now he was outside the superintendent's office, he'd expected to feel angry, but didn't. In fact, he felt nothing at all. Jenny was sat at her computer, typing away. She didn't look up at him as he picked up his coat.

"Uh, Sergeant. I, um, that is, I'm gonna take a week or two off. You'll be in charge of any cases assigned to the team."

She didn't even look up. The old man had always told him never to apologise for your actions or decisions, it was a sign of weakness. He pulled his coat on and turned to leave.

He took one step and then turned back. "Jenny? I'm sorry," he almost whispered. He then turned and walked away.

By the time Jenny looked up, he was already heading toward the door. Had he just...?

Dave was just passing the reception desk when he heard the strange running, clicking footsteps of her high heels behind him. He turned round and saw Jenny thrusting her arms into her coat as she slowed down and walked up to him.

"Sir, I was thinking maybe I could do with a couple of weeks off as well. Uh, if that's okay with you."

He smiled. "Of course, I'll let the Super know I've approved some holiday for you, but I'm not on duty anymore, Sergeant. You can call me Dave if you like."

She smiled warmly. "As long as you call me Jenny."

"Jenny. Would you like to go for a coffee?"

Now she smiled. "I think I'd like that."

Mike felt the hand clasp down heavily on the back of his left shoulder and spin him round so violently that he almost lost his balance and fell to the ground. But he managed to maintain his footing enough to find himself staring at the furious face of the keeper, Jonathon Rawlins. Even though he was outside, Jon was still wearing his robes and gripping his staff. This wasn't good. "That's it, you bastard, you've really done it this time."

Despite shaking and breathing heavily, Mike found himself saying, "Shut up and let go of me; I don't have time for this."

"Get your ass in here right now. I don't care what the vice-mage says, this time you're going to—" Jon's anger was so great that he didn't notice Mike quickly bring his palm up toward the keeper's chest, or the fact that it was glowing. The electricity that Mike had gathered in his hand blasted Jon clean off his feet and slammed him into the wall behind him with such ferocity that it actually knocked the staff out of his hand.

Not stopping to think, Mike turned and ran back toward the university car park without looking back.

Chapter 34

Mike slammed his car door shut and panted as he slumped into the driver's seat. He held up the crucifix and stared at it. He had her! The son of a bitch had her! He had to save her, but how? He needed to find her before it was too late, but how could he? He needed to scry for her and that meant he had to get to her apartment, break in, get something of hers and... Shit, there was no time for that. Jon would be after him any minute now and... "Damn it." He slammed his fists onto the steering wheel.

Suddenly he felt a flash of pain shoot up from his hand, through his arm and into his brain. Almost immediately, he felt fear and panic, but was unable to move or fight and then... It was gone.

He was really out of breath now. He looked down at his open palm and saw Amy's crucifix. It had shown him what was happening to her because it was connected to her, because her soul had rubbed off onto it... Of course, he could scry with this! True, it was a symbol of faith and it should prevent magic, but it was a symbol of Catholic faith. He was Protestant so it wouldn't turn off his power; he could use it to find her!

He wrapped the chain around his right wrist and gripped the piece of sculpted silver in his hand so tightly that it nearly cut into his flesh, but he ignored the pain and discomfort and concentrated, opening his mind.

Normally when he was looking for someone's aura, he needed to be near them to get a fix on their location, but by using a personal possession, he could be any distance away from them.

Anything that was important to someone would inevitably have some of the energy of that person's soul transferred onto it. Mike's psychic power gave him the insight to enable him to use magic to join up the energy on the item with the energy of the individual's soul and effectively create a link to them like a join-the-dots puzzle.

Finally, he opened his eyes and looked ahead of him. He could see the usual grey walls of the car park with his eyes, but he could also see something else, something that wasn't actually there, something in his mind's eye. A glowing ribbon of energy winding through the building and out the exit into the streets. It was constantly twisting, turning and contorting as it wound through the car park and out into the street and with every twist and turn it changed colour: red, yellow, black, blue, purple, every colour imaginable.

Suddenly, Mike felt another sharp pain, this time from his back. "Damn it!" he screamed. He couldn't concentrate; this spell was using too much power. He forced himself to open his eyes again and look ahead through the car windscreen. The energy stream was fading. He closed his eyes once more and fought for concentration. When he opened them again, he could just about see the bright, multicoloured ribbon, but his back felt like it was on fire and a single bead of sweat ran down his forehead.

If he didn't keep his emotions under control he'd lose sight of her aura. He couldn't let that happen; he had to get going. He turned the key in the ignition and revved the car like he'd never revved it before and sped out of the car park, barely stopping to let the barrier open. He drove out onto the road in the direction of the route that the energy stream was leading him.

He was desperately trying hard, despite the pain in his back, to both hold his concentration, and, more importantly, keep the energy visible.

Considering the day she'd just had, Jenny was in a relatively good mood; in fact she was almost ecstatic. She and Dave had just enjoyed a nice coffee at the local cafe and, despite the fact that they barely had the energy to speak much, Dave had invited her back to his place for another drink. She tried to be as coy as possible about accepting the offer but she was finding it hard to contain her excitement. The walk back to his car had been uneventful and so had the drive out of the police station's car park.

It was when they reached the crossroads opposite the university that the small silver Ford Focus screeched out in front of them and nearly cut them up. Even though it was going at a ridiculous pace, they both recognised the driver immediately.

Jenny looked at the expression on Dave's face and her heart sank. She knew they were going to follow that car!

Chapter 35

Teesside was once one of the busiest, noisiest and most polluted counties in the industrial north-east of England. The outskirts of Middlesbrough and its neighbouring town of Stockton once boasted chemical plants, steel works and a huge assortment of supporting industries and companies. Although the chemical industry was still going fairly strong, the steel industry had suffered several setbacks over the years and even though things were starting to look up slightly, it was a little too late for some of the smaller companies. As a result, some of the industrial estates dotted around the area were becoming increasingly empty, like small ghost towns made of concrete and corrugated iron, instead of wood and dirt.

It was one of these industrial estates that Peter Simpkins was now driving into with Kevin Turner. Simpkins had learnt about it several years earlier when he'd been organising funds for new storage facilities for the Order. This estate had the uniqueness of still retaining some working units on the west side, meaning that there was nothing unusual about people driving into the main entrance, while having nothing but empty abandoned buildings on the east side, which meant there was no problem being alone if you needed privacy.

One of these buildings, located at the furthest point east of the estate, was an old, abandoned steel rolling mill that used to produce standard I-beams for the construction industry. It had originally been built during the Industrial Revolution as one of the many rolling mills that used the steel produced by the Dorman Long blast furnaces in Redcar to provide one of the linchpins of the construction boom. Despite surviving past the Revolution and a temporary conversion into a weapons plant during both world wars, the mill could not stop itself from being nationalised into part of British Steel by Harold Wilson's Labour government in 1967. Nor could it prevent itself from being one of several mills that British Steel decommissioned as part of its cost-cutting exercise following its privatisation by Margaret Thatcher's Conservative government in 1988.

Although several of the other decommissioned plants had been bought by developers and subsequently torn down to make way for new housing and offices, this one's location on a still-in-use industrial estate had left it standing as nobody wanted to pay the costs for having it demolished. It had therefore been barricaded up like a fortress after having most of its assets stripped out. All of the main windows had been covered with steel plates and large, heavy industrial-grade steel doors had been secured over the loading bay entrance. Inside, all the machinery had been removed to either be reused at other sites, or sold. The only remnants that had been left behind from the factory's former life were a few desks and chairs in the offices at the back that once held the engineering department. These offices were nothing more than a glorified portacabin that had been constructed on top of the toilet block, accessed by a single set of rickety iron steps, so that the managers could look out onto the factory without having to interact with the workforce.

All of this had made the mill ideal for Simpkins' requirements. Getting past the large padlock on the doors had been no trouble for someone with his skills and the deserted offices were a perfect spot to set up his workshop with all the tools he needed. The large doors that allowed lorries to drive in empty and drive out fully loaded with steel beams now served as the entrance to a convenient car park for himself.

As he now drove up to his wonderful hideaway, he muttered an incantation under his breath and the padlock unhooked itself and the large doors creaked open just enough to allow his vehicle to enter. As always, he pulled the car to one side of the loading area, away from the entrance, so that it couldn't be seen from the outside, and got out. He gripped his staff tightly and told Kevin Turner to get Amy Walsh out of the boot while he fetched the large sheet of cloth he'd left neatly folded in one corner of the factory. Kevin obeyed his command and after removing the still unconscious woman from the car, Simpkins draped the sheet over the vehicle. Once this was done, he led Turner to the back, past the factory floor to the small set of offices at the other end of the mill.

The factory smelt of old oil and stale air. Kevin found his feet were taking him further into the building and he wasn't sure why, or even what was going on. He was barely conscious with no concept of what was happening.

Even though it was still light outside, the factory seemed dark and eerie as most of the high ceiling windows had been plated over with solid steel panels. Only a few untouched panes of glass provided any inkling of light to help him see. A large hole that had once contained the huge machinery that made up the production line cut through the centre of the iron plates that had once been the factory floor like an enormous scar. They walked slowly along the left wall and it was getting increasingly darker as they went further and further into the depths of the mill, until they finally reached the steel steps that led up to the old offices.

After they'd ascended the clanking stairs, Simpkins told Kevin Turner to place Amy Walsh on a chair in the corner of the room that had ornate symbols painted on it. Almost as soon as he placed her in the seat, her head started to stir and she made a groaning sound but this only made Simpkins smile. "Stand back," he told Turner and removed the piece of card with Amy Walsh's hair on it. He gripped it in one hand, and his staff in the other, and called up his will before raising the staff and striking it on the ground whilst crying out, "Bind."

"Shit!" Mike swore as he swerved around a Land Rover that proceeded to beep its horn furiously. He only half-registered the sound and he shoved it almost immediately out of his mind as he continued to focus all of his energy and concentration on his desperate attempt to keep up with the trail of Amy's aura.

He was struggling; the pain in his back was intense. He'd never tried to draw this much power before and he didn't know if he could keep this up for much longer.

He kept chasing the multicoloured energy. It was leading him out of the town and toward one of the industrial areas near Stockton, but he was losing the battle and the energy was fading. But he couldn't give up now. He had to follow it; he had to find her.

* * *

"What the hell is he doing?"

"I don't know, Dave," Jenny answered. She also didn't know what was worrying her more: Michael Walker's driving, Dave's driving, or the really bad feeling that was starting to develop in the pit of her stomach.

Chapter 36

Mike continued to chase the ribbon of energy but it was disappearing fast as he approached the industrial estate. He was running out of strength and it was taking everything he had to keep the link to Amy's aura visible. Hell, it was taking all his strength just to keep his eyes open.

The ribbon of bright light had almost completely vanished as he pulled into the industrial estate. He saw it winding into the east side as it slowly faded into nothing and the pain shooting through his back intensified so much that he had to slam on the brakes. He clamped his eyes shut and fought off the pain. He was so out of breath now that he was panting profusely. Sweat was pouring down his face and dripping down his back. Damn it, there was no time for this. He tried to call up his power again to recreate the link but all he succeeded in doing was causing a huge surge of pain to arch across his back. Shit, he was out of power, but he couldn't lose the trail now.

He slowly peeled his eyes open again and could see some sort of large abandoned factory directly in front of him through his blurry vision. The two huge steel doors were parted just enough to allow a car to enter. Could it be? He pulled his own car up on to a nearby pavement, got out and ran toward the building. Or at least as close to running as his exhausted body would permit.

He entered through the large loading bay door and looked around frantically. Finally, his eyes fell on the large cloth-covered object backed up again the far wall. He dashed over to it and pulled the cloth back to reveal a car. It had to be Simpkins' – he'd found them! But now what? He had no power; how was he going to stop him? He needed help. His hands were shaking now and he was feeling weak.

He fumbled in his pockets, searching for his mobile phone, but he couldn't control his hands properly and get a grip on it. He leant against the vehicle and tried desperately to catch his breath but now his vision was blurring even worse and the room felt like it was spinning. He knew trying to pull that much power was dangerous, but, damn it, he couldn't bail out now. He was now sweating so profusely that his clothes were sticking to him like superglue. Beads of the salty liquid ran down his forehead into his eyes, stinging them, and he felt physically ill. He tried to stand up straight but his legs were getting shaky.

"All right, Walker, what's going on?"

Although shocked to find he wasn't alone, Mike recognised the voice immediately; he'd heard it ask him similar questions for most of the afternoon. He turned around slowly to see Detectives Walsh and Granger standing in the entrance. "Jesus, Walker, what's wrong with you?"

Mike took two unsteady steps forward but it was no good; he was losing the battle. He could barely make out the two figures. "You've got to…"

He saw them coming over to him as he collapsed on the ground. Dust got into his eyes and a strong smell of oil got up his nose but he didn't care. He was too far gone. He felt himself being rolled over and his eyes pulling themselves shut.

He desperately searched for one last burst of strength to raise his hand that still clutched Amy's crucifix and say, "Save her. You've gotta save her." But, as he blacked out, he didn't know if he'd had the strength to say it or not.

Amy suddenly heard someone shout and her eyes opened wide. What the hell was going on? Her head felt like it was throbbing but also it felt like there was a great weight on her entire body, trying to hold her down. She looked down on the chair and saw the glowing sigil and then looked up and saw Simpkins holding his staff with glowing eyes. "No!" she screamed and lunged at him.

Mad Jack was so shocked he nearly dropped his staff, as what he thought was his prize jumped out of the chair straight at him. He was even more shocked when she grabbed hold of him and screamed, "You're not controlling me, you bastard!"

"No!" he screamed back. "Grab her!" Kev grabbed Amy's arms from behind her. She struggled and elbowed him but he seemed to barely register the blows.

"Let go of me!" she screamed. "Kev, what the hell are you doing?" It was then that she turned round and saw the blank look in his eyes and a look of realisation crossed her face. "Oh no! Kev, snap out of it!"

But this pause was all Mad Jack needed to swing his staff down to sweep her feet out from under her. As she fell, Kev grabbed her arms and held them behind her back. As she struggled to regain her footing, Mad Jack raised his staff again and muttered something under his breath. Before Amy knew what was happening, a set of chains that were in the corner of the room suddenly shot through the air and wrapped themselves around her legs and then around her arms before tying themselves together with a horrible, loud clink-clank sound. Kev dropped her to the floor and she swore angrily at them both as the chains rattled and dug into her flesh.

Mad Jack looked down at her. "How can you defy my power without your stupid talisman?"

She looked up at him angrily. "First of all, it's a crucifix, you dummy. Secondly, Mike told me that your tricks only work on the weak-minded and I'm not letting you or anyone else control me. You won't get away with this, you fucking bastards..."

"Shut up, bitch." He turned to Kev and said, "Gag her with something!" Kev reached into his pocket and pulled out a handkerchief, which he stuffed into Amy's mouth, turning her screaming voice into a set of muffled noises.

Mad Jack turned away from them, seething with rage. Nobody defied his power, especially not some unenlightened bitch and her disgraced sorcerer boyfriend. He clenched his fist. Michael Walker. How he wanted to show him who was superior. Then, as he looked out the window back towards the entrance of the factory, he thought he saw something. Could it be?

He turned back towards Kevin Turner. "Sit in the chair," he ordered and the entranced reporter did as he was instructed. Mad Jack slammed his staff on the ground again and yelled, "Bind!" Kevin seemed to go even stiller than he had before. Amy struggled even more to try and yell while wrestling with the chains.

Mad Jack casually stepped over her and removed his balaclava from his pocket before looking back down and saying, "Settle down, bitch. I'll be back to deal with you shortly." He left and slammed the door.

"Sir? Dr Walker? Sir?" Jenny slapped Michael Walker gently on the face but he didn't respond. She flipped out her mobile phone and dialled 999. "Hello, this is Detective Sergeant... Hello? Hello?" She looked at the screen frantically. "Shit, there's no signal, we've got to get him—"

Suddenly she heard an almighty crash followed by a loud click and spun around just in time to see that the two huge metal doors had slammed shut. She ran up to them and pushed but they were locked securely from the outside! She banged on them fruitlessly and screamed for help but nobody answered and they refused to budge. The doors had now cut off what was virtually the only source of light, so she felt along the cold, smooth steel until finally she felt the roughness of the brick under her fingers. Eventually, she came across some sort of control panel. She frantically pushed and pulled various levers, switches and buttons but it was no good – the lights refused to switch on.

"What the hell is going on here?"

Using her phone as a light source, she turned back and was shocked to find Dave shaking the now unconscious Michael Walker frantically. "Where is she?" he was demanding. "What the hell's happened to her?"

"Dave, look out."

In the darkness, the bright light of the fireball stood out like Blackpool Illuminations, but Dave's back was to it and he wouldn't have seen it in time. Jenny dived and managed to push both him and Michael Walker out of the way just as the flame slammed onto the ground that they'd been occupying and erupted with a huge explosion.

"What the hell?"

A strange creepy laughter started to echo around the old factory.

"Who's there?" Dave demanded.

Another ball of fire exploded out of the darkness straight at them. Dave shoved Jenny to one side and rolled himself in the other direction, hoping to separate them so they were harder to attack, but he tripped over Michael Walker's still body and landed head first onto the car's bumper.

Jenny watched, horrified, as he lay flat on the floor. The second ball of fire brought some more light to the empty building and now she could just about make out the outline of a lone figure stepping out of the darkness and approaching her menacingly.

She tried to stand but when Dave had pushed her aside, she'd got tangled in some discarded cables that were laying on the floor. She tried desperately to free herself but found that she couldn't. It was almost as if the cables were gripping her tighter as she fought against them. The figure stepped over. He was wearing a long coat, his face was obscured by a pitch-black balaclava, and he was carrying a long piece of wood that seemed to be smouldering.

Jenny gulped. "It's you, isn't it?" she screamed. "You're Mad Jack."

The figure laughed as he raised his staff.

Chapter 37

Amy twisted and struggled against the chains that held her, but the double knot they'd tied themselves into was behind her bound arms and there was nothing she could do to reach it, no matter how much she tried. She desperately looked up at Kev and tried to scream at him, but not only was her mouth muffled but Kev was completely still and motionless. She guessed that the circle somehow contained energy from the spirit world so that Simpkins wouldn't waste all the power in his staff to hold someone in place. A part of her supposed that she could at least be proud that her last thought had been a smart one, especially considering what an idiot she'd been to have gotten herself into this damn mess.

Desperately, she looked around the room for something, anything, that could be used. Then she saw that she was next to an old wooden desk, which had a nail sticking out of it. Struggling around, she managed to crawl over to it and propped herself up enough to snag the end of the handkerchief on the exposed nail and leaned back so that it was pulled out of her mouth.

She gasped and turned back around and crawled toward the chair. "Kev!" she screamed as she swung round on her butt to kick the chair. "Snap out of it, you moro—" Before she could finish the sentence, her legs hit an invisible wall of force, knocking her back.

Kev remained completely still. She propped herself back up and looked up at him. The stupid bugger. For a while, all she could think about were all the good times the two of them had spent together.

Then she started to think of Mike Walker. Less than a week ago they'd never even met, but in that short time he'd turned her entire world upside down. He'd saved her life, showed her a secret world of magic and even taught her how to do magic herself.

Her eyes snapped open. The magic. Could she?

She closed her eyes again and looked within herself like Mike had showed her. Amazingly, she was able to find her power. She tried to push it out of herself in an attempt to break the chains but it did nothing. "Shit," she swore as she opened her eyes. Of course it didn't work; she'd need to know how to use her power to do alchemy like Mike showed her. But she was desperate, so she tried again and pushed further this time. Again, the chains didn't even flinch but this time she felt something else outside her body, almost as if her power was knocking into another power. She opened her eyes and realised that she was still near the chair. Wait a minute, maybe she could use her power to break whatever was holding Kev and then he could free her.

With a bit of twisting, she managed to get herself sat up and carefully shuffled herself as close as she dared to what she thought was the force field that blasted her. Once more, she closed her eyes and drew up her power and soon felt it pushing against the magic of the chair. She tried desperately to push her own power against it but it refused to budge. She refused to give up; this was her only hope and she couldn't just submit to defeat.

Suddenly, she stopped as she heard a moan. She snapped her eyes open again and looked up at Kev; she swore she saw his lip tremble and his eyes blink. "Kev?" As she said his name, she swore she saw him move again slightly. What was it that Mike had told her? *Your name has power and can be used as a vessel to transfer power to you?* Maybe if she said Kev's name while using her own power on the barrier she could transfer some of it to him and break the spell he was under. She closed her eyes once more and quickly drew up her power again. She pushed at it with all her power's might, feeling intense pressure from the barrier.

Please, God, let this work, she thought, and then screamed, "Kevin Turner!" She blasted forward as the chair fell to the floor.

Chapter 38

"You bitch!" Mad Jack swore as he swung the staff like a club for a second time. Jenny managed to just roll out of the way of the blow, despite being somehow tangled up in the mass of electrical cables. She twisted around and propped herself up on her left hand. Desperately, she reached around her back to grasp hold of her collapsible truncheon, but she only managed to get her hand tangled up in the cables. She struggled further but then somehow her other hand got tangled up as well. She lost her balance and fell back down on her knees with a painful thud.

She scrambled frantically to try and free herself but the cables seemed to keep re-tangling themselves around her legs and then her arms, then suddenly she realised one of the cables was somehow around her neck! How the hell was that possible? Panic was setting in now. She felt her throat being constricted as she gasped for air. Desperately, she struggled and finally managed to get her arms somewhat untangled and squeezed her fingers between the cable and her throat. The tough insulation felt cold and stiff as it pressed against her neck and fingers, cutting off her circulation and crushing her neck. It was then that she saw Mad Jack was just standing there, clutching his staff and muttering to himself. Horrid realisation started to creep through her.

"What the hell are you?" she screeched.

The man just continued his strange chanting as a horrible, wicked smile spread across his lips – the only thing besides his bright, pale eyes visible through the balaclava he wore.

The fire was growing now; whatever he'd used to blast them with was spreading. Despite the pain, Jenny suddenly had a horrible thought: this place was probably soaked in oil, leftover from its operational days. The fire could grow into a raging inferno! She looked over frantically at the two still bodies. Wait, there wasn't two still bodies, there was only one; where was...?

Despite the roar of the flames, she suddenly heard an ear-splitting crack followed by an equally ear-splitting scream. She looked back up quickly to find that Dave was up and had just brought his own truncheon straight across Mad Jack's back. She fought against her bonds once more and found that she was now able to wriggle free of them. She gasped as she twisted and turned before finally being able to fling the cables away. Quickly she scrambled to her feet and reached for her own truncheon.

Jack was attacking Dave like the madman he was, using that weird stick he'd been carrying like a club and swinging at the inspector wildly. Dave was desperately trying to parry the blows with his truncheon but he was still unsteady on his feet from the knock he'd taken to his head. Jenny lunged, but she'd underestimated Mad Jack. He'd been keeping half an eye on her and made a sudden jump to his right and she slammed head first into Dave, taking them both tumbling to the floor. They both twisted round to see Jack running away from the inferno and into the darkness of the factory.

"We've got to follow him," Jen yelled with a cough; the fumes were really starting to build up now. "He must know another way out."

Dave nodded groggily and got up. They made a dash for Michael Walker, but he was gone.

"Where...?"

Suddenly, another fireball roared through the air and slammed into the wall behind them, followed by horrible cackling laughter. The heat was starting to get intense and oily smoke started to choke their lungs. They tried to head the way Jack had gone but almost as soon as they started to move, another ball of flame erupted out of the darkness. But this one wasn't aimed at them; it was shooting straight upwards. It hit the ceiling and part of the roof fell in with a crash so loud Jenny thought she'd gone deaf. A mass of tangled steel and corrugated iron now cut them off from Mad Jack's escape route.

Then a momentous roar erupted. Suddenly, the large machinery hole that cut through the centre of the factory erupted in a mass of flame. Something that had been left behind from the days of the factory's operation had caught fire and exploded.

Dave and Jenny looked around in panic, but all their exits were now blocked; they were trapped.

Chapter 39

Kev blinked two or three times. He felt like he'd been asleep for weeks but found himself laying on a cold, hard floor in a room that stank of oil and moisture damage. He slowly propped himself up and shook his head. What the hell had happened to him? He looked around and saw the still body lying on the other side of the room. It took him half a second to recognise her.

"Oh my God. Amy," he yelled, stumbling over to her. "What happened? Amy!" She stirred but only slightly. "Amy!" he screamed. He thought he heard something. "Amy!" He was sure it was a groan.

Amy felt nothing. She wondered if this was what death felt like. Then she remembered that she'd thought that once before; the time she'd first met Mike Walker and Mad Jack. When Mike had saved her life. Mike! Was she ever going to see him again?

Then she heard it. It was her name. Someone was saying her name, she was sure of it. It was then that she felt something; it was cold and hard beneath her. Wait a minute, if she could feel something then that meant she was alive. Was she breathing? Yes, she was!

She attempted to open her eyes. It was difficult, almost as if she didn't have the energy to do it. What the hell had she done? She tried again. This time she was able to open them but her vision was fuzzy. Where was she?

"Amy! Hang on, I'll get these things off you."

She heard the clink and clank of metal and realised that she could move slightly easier as the chains around her were being pulled off. "What... What happened?" she said as her vision came back into focus.

"I don't know," Kev said. "But I think we need to get out of here." As he removed the last chain, he asked, "Can you get up?"

"Uh, I think so," she said, though it turned out her feet were more than a little unsteady and she found herself collapsing to one knee and panting. Kev said something else, something about smelling smoke, but she didn't really listen. Then he said something else again, something about hearing footsteps.

The door burst open and he strode in. He was dragging someone else behind him. Amy looked up. Despite her drained state, she still recognised the still figure who lay as limp as a rag in Simpkins' grip.

"No, please, no!" she screamed.

A look of fury crept over Simpkins' face as he stared at them. He dropped the still body of Mike Walker on the floor next to him, between the two desks that stood either side of the doorway, before stepping forward and slowly raising his staff.

He was almost upon them when Kev finally found his backbone. "Keep away from her, you son of a bitch!" he screamed as he drew himself up to his full height.

Simpkins barely blinked as he swung the staff at Kev who amazingly managed to grab it and pushed the small man back. As the two started to tussle, Amy wasted no time and crawled as fast as she could over to Mike's still form. "Mike! Mike!" she screamed. "Speak to me. Speak to me." Mike didn't stir but she heard a clatter behind her and looked up to see Simpkins and Kev locked in a fierce struggle. She looked back down at Mike and checked for a pulse. Thank God, she found one, but it was faint. She closed her eyes and drew up her power once more and reached out for Mike's own aura. She was amazed that she not only found it but recognised it immediately, but it was faint. No, she couldn't lose him. She needed him.

Kev had got a couple of punches in but when he took a fierce swing at Simpkins he missed and lost his footing. The insane treasurer immediately took the opportunity to knee Kev squarely in the stomach. Kevin gasped as the wind was knocked completely out of him and Simpkins gave him a single, swift hit over the head with his staff, connecting solidly with a single dull thud. Kev slumped to the floor like a sack of potatoes and he moved no more.

Simpkins casually took off the balaclava he was wearing and turned to look down at Amy with the coldest, emptiest eyes she'd ever seen and then he smiled wickedly. "Well, my dear, I think it's time I took my prize." Out of his coat pocket he produced the same kitchen knife that he'd held against her throat that wet, rainy night two weeks ago. Amy eyes grew in horror.

She looked down at the still figure laying on the floor and knew exactly what she had to do. Closing her eyes and reaching out with her power to touch his aura, desperately she screamed two final words. "Michael Walker!" Then everything faded into nothing.

Chapter 40

Darkness, nothing but darkness.

Then a light, he heard a light.

How could he hear a light?

Suddenly he was aware again.

He had a body, arms, legs, a head, eyes…

He opened the eyes and the first thing that he saw was Amy laying totally still in front of him but then he saw past her.

"You!" Mike screamed at Simpkins without thinking.

The small man stared at him in disbelief. "You're still alive?" he hissed in disgust before whipping around and aiming his staff directly at Mike's head. Mike froze with fear; he had to move but he was still too weak and his body felt like it was covered in bruises, as if he'd been dragged up a set of stairs backwards. He needed to roll to one side to avoid the blast but a desk on either side of the small doorway blocked his escape. Simpkins eyes had already glazed over into perfectly white pearls and he was starting to chant his incantation. Without thinking, Mike dived forward and covered Amy's body.

"Firara, Firugo!" Simpkins screamed and the tip of the staff smouldered.

Mike clamped his eyes shut and covered his face with his hands, hoping it would offer them some protection as he braced for the blast's impact. He waited for the pain to come, but he felt nothing. In fact, he didn't even feel any heat, but he did smell smoke. He lowered his arms and opened his eyes; Simpkins was standing there, shaking his staff up and down furiously.

He aimed it at Mike again and repeated the incantation, "Firara, Firugo." But, once again, no fire came out, just a small puff of smoke!

The sudden burst of fear had started the adrenaline pumping through his body and Mike found he had enough strength now to push himself up on his hands to stare at the insane treasurer. Then he pretended to laugh. "What's the matter? Out of juice?" he asked.

Simpkins snarled. Mike managed to reach up and use the two desks that he was laying in between to lever himself up onto his feet, though he still felt unsteady. His body ached and he was still drained; he knew trying to call up any power would be suicidal. He looked at Simpkins. The little man looked different. For the first time since Mike had met him, he wasn't wearing a tie. The long grey coat he wore clashed with his now grubby yellow shirt and brown trousers but that wasn't the main difference. Simpkins' entire demeanour had changed; he wasn't hunched and nervous anymore. He looked like a caged animal that had just been set free: wild, hungry and dangerous.

The two men stood there, staring at each other with equal dislike, sizing each other up and wondering what the other would do next. It was then that Mike looked past Simpkins and saw the unconscious body of another man. Almost immediately, his eyes looked back down at Amy's completely still body lying there on the floor. Anger boiled into him so quickly that he didn't even think to be afraid anymore. Without even considering the consequences, he looked Simpkins straight in the eye. "What have you done to her, you bastard?"

Simpkins inhaled. "Nothing yet." His voice sounded different too; it wasn't nervous anymore. It was deep, hollow and filled with anger. "But I will. Nobody defies my power."

"Oh, really?" Mike found himself saying. "You could have fooled me." The bald man's face went red, but Mike couldn't stop. "Y'know it's amazing, Amy's profile was spot on. You are a shite wizard, as well as being an evil bastard!" The effect was instantaneous; Simpkins screamed in anger and lunged forward. It was only then that Mike noticed the knife that was in his other hand. "Aw, bollocks!"

Mike was no expert in self-defence, but it was at that moment he learnt how it was amazing what you can do when your life is threatened. Instinctively he sidestepped away from the knife and grabbed Simpkins' wrists and tried to push him back. Simpkins was shaking like a madman and desperately trying to stab Mike with his right hand or beat him with the staff in his left hand. His eyes were glazed over, but it wasn't from trying to cast a spell; it was from sheer madness. Mike was still weak, and it was only his increased height over Simpkins that allowed him to step over Amy and keep the lunatic from reaching him.

Suddenly Mike started to feel the heat on his back and he smelt more smoke, but neither was coming from Simpkins' staff. He risked a furtive glance behind him and saw the huge, thick flames of the growing inferno and the thick, black smoke spreading throughout the factory. Oh God, what the hell had happened? Where were those two coppers?

Mike snapped his head back round quickly. Simpkins' insanity seemed to be intensifying and with it, the intensity of his onslaught. He was now desperately trying to kick Mike, but his small legs couldn't quite reach him. It was then that Mike knew what he had to do; he lashed out with a kick of his own. Simpkins legs may have been too short to reach, but Mike's were more than long enough to connect squarely, right where they would hurt the little man the most – right between his legs!

Simpkins screamed in agony and dropped both his weapons. Almost instinctively, Mike pulled the treasurer toward himself and slammed his knee into the insane wizard's stomach, knocking the wind out of him. Without stopping for a second, Mike released his grip and put all his rage and anger into an incredibly fierce punch to Simpkins' face, flooring him. He waited for Simpkins to stir, but the lunatic lay still.

Mike stood there for a few seconds, panting and catching his breath, then he dashed back over to where Amy was laying. He carefully moved her away from the desks into a clear part of the floor and bent down to touch her neck. She had a pulse, but, oh, God! He looked around frantically; he saw the symbols burnt into the floor next to the turned over chair. Oh no. Suddenly, he realised what must have happened. She must have tried to use the power of her soul to break Simpkins' trapping spell, but she'd overexerted herself and drained too much energy. If she'd used up too much power, she could have caused permanent damage to her soul and that meant... Oh, God!

What had she done?

What had he done?

He'd taught her sorcery without teaching her the consequences or dangers. She didn't know that most people only had a certain amount of power in their soul and that when that was used up...!

He looked around frantically for inspiration and, just in time, saw Simpkins jumping and lunging at him again. The son of a bitch was playing possum!

Mike was knocked to the floor. He twisted and turned, trying to get Simpkins off him. They rolled all over the room, banging into the walls and knocking over furniture. Mike didn't register the noise of all the clattering or even the bruising of his body. It was all happening so fast. Suddenly, he found himself on his back with Simpkins knelt on his chest pinning him down. The treasurer thrust his hands out and gripped Mike by the throat. Mike looked up at him; he almost couldn't believe it, the small man was literally foaming at the mouth. His eyes were so bloodshot that they didn't even look human.

Mike coughed and spluttered and flailed around widely in panic. He tried to gather his power, but he was so weak all he succeeded in doing was causing more pain to shoot through his back. He desperately looked round for inspiration, and though smoke was gathering over his head, Mike could just about make out the shape of the man on the floor somewhere behind Simpkins. That meant they were directly in front of the door. What could he do?

He had to do something.

Simpkins was choking him to death.

But he was out power, out of strength, out of hope, out of faith.

His eyes widened. Faith! That was it!

Simpkins' grip on his throat was unrelenting. Mike was starting to feel dizzy as he clawed and gripped at the madman's hands. He knew he only had one chance as he swung his right arm out and slammed his fist into Simpkins' left hand. Simpkins may have been expecting that, but he clearly wasn't expecting the sudden sharp pain it brought him! Mike quickly removed his own hand and the madman screamed and released his grip on Mike's throat so that he could instinctively grab his suddenly bleeding left hand with his right one. The warm, sticky, red fluid seeped through his fingers as it oozed out of the hole. Mike seized the opportunity and, remembering an old judo move he'd once seen on television, not to mention the basic laws of physics, he reached up, grabbed hold of Simpkins' shirt and rolled backwards, raising his legs to transfer all the momentum from the roll into the treasurer, hurtling the small man through the still open door.

Mike heard the piercing, high-pitched scream, followed by an almighty crash and then an even louder scream that sounded like it was coming from something that wasn't human. He twisted himself around, coughing and spluttering while clutching his painful neck. Without thinking, he dashed over to the door and out onto the iron landing, instantly realising that he wasn't on the ground floor anymore. He grabbed onto the single iron guardrail for support against the sudden sense of vertigo he was feeling and cautiously peered down over the edge. His eyes widened in horror as he looked over the railing, down into the factory.

Simpkins was on fire!

He'd fallen off the small metal balcony into the huge hole in the factory floor, landing directly into the spreading inferno. He must have broken more than a few bones as he seemed unable to stand and was rolling around, back and forth, like he was trying to put out the flames but was just rolling himself into more and more of the fire, seeming to have lost all sense of direction and any semblance of sanity.

Mike turned and started to run down the stairs but a huge sheet of flame erupted at the base of them, causing him to stop so suddenly that he almost fell backwards and had to grab the handrail to steady himself.

The pain ripped through him and he screamed furiously at himself. The first one had screamed the same way when he'd finished with him. That smarmy salesman who'd reminded him so much of his damn brother. All he'd wanted was to get a car: he didn't want a bloody pal. Especially not one like him; so smarmy, so arrogant, so full of himself, so... Confident!

After he'd left the place he couldn't stop thinking about the unenlightened fool. He'd been so chummy, slapping him on the back like he owned him, just like his brother did, like he knew it all! The unenlightened fool. Still, he'd shown him. When he went back later and surprised him, he knew his name, he could control him, that was all he wanted to prove. He just took the knife for protection, but the fool dared to defy him, defy his power, but he'd shown him. He'd shown him who was superior.

Then he'd been walking in the park and saw another fool just like him, with that marvellous prize. He didn't deserve her; why did they always go with those worthless fools? He deserved her, not that fool. So he took her and showed both of them. He'd shown her and him who was best.

He'd shown them all!

He'd shown them who was superior!

He'd shown them who was the best!

He was superior!

He was the best!

Nobody defied his power!

He screamed again, one final time.

The heat was so intense that Mike was trapped. He looked down over the guardrail, leaning against it for support as he watched the man who had killed two of his students rolling backwards and forwards within the increasingly ferocious flames that were spreading through the factory floor. He didn't want to look, but for some reason he found that he couldn't look away either. Then, suddenly, Simpkins stopped rolling; the large sprawling fiery mass that he'd become twitched uncontrollably for a short time and was then perfectly still.

The smell of burning flesh started to creep into Mike's nostrils, making him feel sick. He winced slightly and covered his mouth but he still continued to stare at the lifeless corpse burning as he coughed and spluttered from the smoke.

He couldn't save Simpkins.

He couldn't save Amy.

He couldn't save himself.

He looked down into his hand at Amy's blood-stained crucifix with its chain still wrapped round his wrist and wondered if faith could save them now.

Chapter 41

Dave and Jenny lay flat on their stomachs, desperately trying to breathe amid the ever increasing smoke and fire. Both were continuously looking around, searching for some way of escape. There were no other exits; the windows were too high and the collapsed roof cut them off from the rest of the factory.

Dave looked over at Jenny through smoke-reddened eyes. "Jen." She looked over at him through eyes that were equally as red and equally as teary. "I'm sorry. I'm really sorry. For everything."

Amazingly, Jenny managed to smile. She reached out and took his hand. "It's okay , Dave, it's okay "

He smiled as well and leaned closer to her. She leaned over and they were almost nose to nose when they heard an almighty crash above them. They looked up sharply and saw the glass from one of the few windows that hadn't been sealed up falling down around them. Quickly, they covered their faces to protect themselves from the falling shards. They strained to look through the smoke; Dave saw nothing, but Jenny could have sworn that she saw the outline of a huge bird flying into the factory.

Mike coughed and spluttered as he piled the last chair on top of the desk that he'd managed to push against the doorway. He'd foolishly hoped that he could create some sort of barricade to keep out as much of the smoke as possible. His thinking at the time was that if he could keep the fire out of the room long enough, then he could rest and regain enough of his strength to be able to use his power to escape. What an idiot he'd been; he was a physicist, for God's sake, he knew all about smoke dispersion.

He pulled out his phone again and tried once more to desperately get a signal and call for help, but it was no good. The display showed no bars and every time he pressed the call button all he got was an irritating beep accompanied by a message of 'No Network' on the screen. He ran around every corner of the room and reached up high with the phone, but every time he tapped the screen, he got the same response. Either there were no towers nearby, which was unlikely, or Simpkins had set up some sort of dampening spell around the building, which was even more unlikely.

Eventually he gave up and shoved the phone back in his pocket before pulling out a handkerchief to cover his face and dashing back over to Amy and the unconscious man – Mike had had no luck in rousing him. The poor bloke had suffered a nasty blow to the head and was probably suffering from some sort of concussion. Mike suddenly wished that he hadn't passed over that opportunity to become a first-aider at work.

He lent down by Amy once more and tried again to call up his power so that he could share some of it with her and maybe heal her soul, but it was no good. The pain in his back merely increased.

"Damn you, Jon!" he screamed.

"Anger like that will not help you now, Michael Walker."

Mike looked up sharply at his makeshift barricade. Perched on top of it was a huge bird with magnificent bright red feathers. He recognised it immediately. "You're..."

"Yes, Michael. I am Rox. Jonathon Rawlins is my master. Tell me, where is Peter Simpkins?"

Mike pointed behind him and the phoenix flew into the main factory. "Wait!" But it was already gone. Mike dashed up to the barricade and desperately tore away the chairs to peer out but he needn't have bothered. Almost immediately, Rox reappeared at the door once more.

"I shall carry you out, Michael."

"Wait, there are other people trapped in here."

"They will be taken care of."

Before Mike could protest, Rox grabbed his shoulders with his claw-like feet, dragged him through the doorway and flew into the air. Mike covered his face and screamed as the phoenix crashed through the only remaining glass window in the roof of the factory and flew out into the fresh air.

Dave's eyes felt heavy; he thought he was losing his battle to keep conscious. The smoke seamed to worsen and the darkness was getting thicker. Then suddenly he heard a loud metallic bang. He looked for the source of the noise; it was coming from the large metal doors. Then suddenly, from the centre, a thin crack of light appeared and started to expand slightly. Someone was trying to pry them open!

"HELP! We're in here!" Dave screamed.

It was then that he noticed that Jenny wasn't shouting with him. He looked over at her. Her eyes were closed!

"HELP! For God's sake, get us out of here!"

Dave heard a metallic clunk and something poked through the open crack, a lever of some sort, maybe a crowbar. It bent to the right and then, slowly, the light grew larger as someone began prying the two doors apart.

"Over here!" he started screaming. Slowly, the doors opened enough to let a single figure squeeze through. When Dave saw who was coming to their rescue, a part of him wished he'd kept his mouth shut.

Mike watched as the man he would later learn was Chief Inspector Frank Williams and his people carried Amy out of the rolling mill and place her into the waiting ambulance, just as they'd done with the two coppers and the other man he would come to know was Amy's ex-boyfriend, Kevin Turner, the journalist.

In the time that it had taken Williams to get the detectives out of the factory, the fire brigade had somehow managed to get the flames under control enough for them to get further in and retrieve Amy and Kevin.

The four victims were placed into two ambulances and driven away; the fifth person to be brought out wasn't so lucky. Mike was relieved to see that they'd covered Simpkins' lifeless body in a cloth. He really didn't want to see what had happened to the insane treasurer.

"Right, you've seen that they're okay. Now let's get going. I can't keep this veil up forever."

"You're a real humanitarian, Jon." Mike closed the window of the black BMW that Rox had dropped him into. Guess the Order was doing good business these days to afford such a nice set of wheels for a keeper. "How did the police and fire brigade get here?"

"They received an anonymous tip-off," Jon replied as he released the veil from around the car and laid his staff down beside him before starting the engine.

"What about my car?" Mike asked as he rubbed his forehead.

"One of my fellow keepers has dealt with it. To the unenlightened, it will seem like you were never here." Mike whistled through his teeth. "Are you at least going to thank me?" Jon asked without taking his eyes off the road for a second as he drove them out of the estate.

Mike looked over at the keeper. "Thank you for the fact that you came here to have the pleasure of finishing me off yourself?"

Jon sniffed. "You're not to be finished off."

Mike looked up sharply. "Say what?"

Jon gritted his teeth. "You were right," he grunted.

Chapter 42

Jon drove Mike round the back of the Order and pulled the car in front of one of the blank walls at the end of the row of white terrace houses. The keeper placed his hand on an ornate sigel that had been painted onto the car's dashboard in what looked like whitewash. It glowed brightly under his palm and, almost immediately, the wall in front of them shimmered and contorted until an entrance large enough for the vehicle to pass through appeared.

Jon then drove the car into the newly created entrance and down a ramp that led into an underground car park. The entrance vanished as Jon parked his vehicle and gestured for Mike to go with him. He followed the keeper into a small lift at the back of the building. The walls, ceiling and floor of the lift were all made of a soft, plush, bright red velvet and there was no control panel. Jon merely waved his staff to cause the doors to close themselves and the lift to start rising.

The two men hadn't said anything to each other the whole way back and Mike was wondering what the hell was going on. The keeper just stared straight ahead and didn't even give Mike a sideways glance. The ice-cold bastard.

The lift was going so high that they must have been heading to the living apartments on one of the top floors where some of the Order's permanent staff kept residence. Finally, the lift jolted to a halt and the doors opened silently. Jon gestured Mike out. He stepped into the hallway suspiciously, letting Jon lead the way down the corridor until they stopped outside one of the many oak doors that lined the wall. These doors were almost identical to the office ones downstairs except that they each had a small, brass plate affixed to them.

Mike's eyes widened. The nameplate on the door they were approaching read, 'P Simpkins'. Jon flicked his staff and the door creaked opened. Mike followed the keeper inside to find a room that was probably best described as spartan. There was one chair, one desk, no photos, no pictures, no television and no light bulbs. The only light in the dark, eerie room came from a few old-fashioned oil lamps dotted about it with their flames licking the air.

A lone figure was standing with his back to the door as Mike and Jon entered, but Mike could tell immediately who it was from the long staff that he clutched in his right hand, with its red orb glowing brightly in the dimly lit room.

"Would you please leave us alone, Keeper Rawlins?" the vice-mage asked calmly without turning round to face them. Jon looked at Mike and sniffed disapprovingly before leaving and closing the door behind him.

"Well?" Mike asked. "Am I to be dealt with or not?" Chris was silent. "I'm not, am I?"

"You were right," was all his old mentor said in reply.

"Sorry?" Mike tried hard not to be too surprised or sarcastic. Chris had never admitted to anyone else about them being right about anything, even if he agreed with what they were right about! It was then that Mike realised exactly what Chris was saying. "How do you know...?"

Without turning around, Chris pointed behind him. Mike turned around slowly and looked with horror at what was on the lone simple, wooden bookshelf erected on the back wall. Seven jars, all lined up in a perfectly straight row with identically sized, neatly printed hand-written labels. Each one contained, something... It wasn't tangible, but it was there, some sort of energy that looked like a constantly changing mass: no form, no texture, not solid, but still something visible. As Mike looked at them, they kept changing colour: red, blue, green, yellow, every colour he could think of and some that he couldn't even name. Although they all looked to be the same substance, no two had the same formless shape; they were all... unique. Suddenly, Mike realised exactly what he was looking at: they'd found Simpkins' trophies.

"Oh my God." Mike's hand covered his face. "He took their souls!"

"When you were so desperate to find Mr Simpkins and handled Keeper Rawlins so brazenly, I knew there must have been something seriously wrong so I persuaded Jonathon to open this apartment so that we could investigate. It was then that we found them."

Mike stared at the jars in disbelief. He'd heard that it was possible to extract a person's soul (and hence their mind) at the time of their death and then contain it by use of a spell imprinted on a container using symbology, but he never thought that anyone would be so depraved as to try it, let alone use it repeatedly!

Chris turned around slowly and walked behind him. "Your behaviour was still totally unacceptable,

Michael." His voice was the same stern one that Mike used to hear every day when he was still an apprentice, but then Chris softened it slightly. "But I've managed to convince Keeper Rawlins that it wouldn't be prudent for him to pursue his... issues with yourself."

"Thanks."

"Provided you do not make too much about this unfortunate business."

Mike snorted. "You mean as long as I don't let anyone know that you allowed this to happen on your patch?" Chris was silent. Mike sighed. "So what happens now?"

"Things have been arranged so that the... proper authorities, who found Mr Simpkins' body, will realise the terrible things that he's done without having to come here and disturb our ways."

"Amy's criminal profile."

"Sorry?"

"Amy Walsh – the woman who he'd kidnapped in the factory. She's a psychologist who was hired by the police to produce a criminal profile on Mad Jack. You'll find that it describes Simpkins to a tee."

Chris was silent for a brief moment. "Yes, very good, that coupled with your map should be enough."

"You mean my geographic profile."

"Yes, that."

Mike sighed then closed his eyes for a second. "What about these?"

Chris sighed. "The jars will have to be destroyed so that they can move on." Again, he paused. "I thought you may want a moment with the last one before..."

"The last two."

"Sorry?"

"The last two were both my students. He killed the last one just the other day."

"Michael, I..." Chris trailed off. "I'll leave you for a moment."

"I'm weak, Chris." The vice-mage said nothing but Mike felt him press the orb of his staff against his back. Slowly the orb started to warm up and Mike felt the power flow out from the staff and into himself. He soon felt his own power completely replenish and Chris removed the orb from his back. He heard his old mentor walk away and the door close behind him as he left the room.

Walking over to the bookshelf, Mike picked up the last two jars and took them over to the small desk that was set up in the other corner of the room. The labels on the jars read simply Kerry and Tracy. Circles containing identical symbols had been painted on top of each of the lids in a thick black substance with a horrible strong smell; if Mike didn't know better he'd have sworn that it was creosote.

Well it was no good putting this off. He sighed heavily and placed his hands over the symbols on the lids. The ward used in the seals were almost identical to the one Simpkins had on his office door and he soon found the weak spot. He closed his eyes and opened his mind.

In his psyche, he opened his eyes and found himself standing in an empty void. There was nothing around him but darkness, endless darkness. He should have been falling, but he stood straighter and taller than he ever did in real life.

Then, as he gently lowered his psychic defences, two formless masses of glowing white energy began to slowly materialise in front of him. Then, gradually, they started to mould and shape themselves into humanoid figures, gradually taking on the form of his two dead students, right down to the clothes they last wore. At first they looked terrified, then confused, then, when they finally saw Mike, a strange look of surprised realisation crossed their faces.

Mike turned to Kerry first. "I'm so sorry. I wish there was something I could have done to stop him. I know it's a small consolation but he's gone now, he won't harm anyone else, I promise. I'm so sorry for you and your parents." They couldn't speak but before he could see the expression on Kerry's face he turned to Tracy. "I really am so sorry. I screwed up. All I can say is that I promise I'll make sure that your research is published under your name. I'm so sorry for you and your family."

He tried not to look at them but he couldn't help but see the pain and realisation on their faces; he was certain that if they could, they would have both cried. He'd screwed up again. He couldn't even get this right; he couldn't even just say goodbye correctly. He needed to get this over with; there was nothing more he could do. He dropped his head. "It's time. I'm sorry." He felt the pressure and when he looked up again, the two figures were gone.

He opened his real eyes and found himself back in Simpkins' room. He looked down at the crushed jars beneath his hands. Small puffs of multicoloured smoke were quickly fading away from beneath his fists.

"Rest in peace. God bless you." He turned to the bookshelf. "All of you."

He raised his hand, flicked it and the bookshelf collapsed. He watched the remaining five jars smash as they hit the floor and the energy rose from them into the air in a rainbow of colours and then faded away into nothing like it was the last remnants of the smoke from a dying fire. He bowed his head and said a prayer under his breath. He felt the tears trickling down his face and wiped them away with the back of his hand before leaving the room.

Chris and Jon were standing on either side of the door when he exited. He nodded at Chris, who nodded back solemnly. He looked up at Jon and nodded, but the keeper remained still. Mike was about halfway toward the lift when he stopped and turned back to Jon. "Uh, sorry about the electric shock."

The keeper just sniffed but Mike could have sworn Chris nearly snickered under his breath. Not wanting to antagonise the keeper any further, Mike just gave a sheepish half-smile and dashed through the lift's doors. He waved his hand to make them close and the container started to descend. He knew that really he should stay and help clean up the mess he'd just made, but he couldn't waste time. There was something he had to do.

Epilogue

Mike waited until late that night. Eventually all the visitors were made to leave and he was alone. He'd stayed in the hospital waiting room until they were ushering everyone out before he called up his power and twirled his fingers to raise a veil around himself. Once he was sure the last of the visitors were gone, he stood up from the uncomfortable, hard, plastic visitors' chair and headed toward the wards. Nobody noticed him as he walked through the hallway. He gripped the crucifix in his left hand and gently ebbed just enough power out to allow him to create a small faint trail of her aura. He followed the image of constantly changing multicoloured energy until finally he found himself stood outside a private room.

He released both spells, took a deep breath and walked in. She was lying on a hospital bed that had a thin mattress and handrails. Someone had undressed her and put her into one of those cheap, disposable, pale blue hospital gowns that looked like they were made of paper.

He stood next to the bed and looked down at her. Despite all the tubes and monitoring equipment they'd connected up to her, she still looked so peaceful, so vulnerable, so beautiful. He took her right hand in his own, closed his eyes and concentrated. He opened his mind and searched within her until finally he found the remaining energy of her badly depleted soul. He latched onto that energy, drew up his own power and started to let as much of it flow into her as possible. Desperately, he tried to fuse the two together. Finally he succeeded and after a lot of effort, he had the two powers completely intertwined. Then he started to pour more and more of his own energy into hers. He pushed himself to his absolute limit, until he felt the pain in his back, but he tried his best to ignore it as he pushed on further past his normal limit until he was sure that her soul was restored to its original strength.

Finally, he released his grip and the small amount of energy he kept for himself snapped off the rest that he left behind for her. He looked down hopefully, but she remained completely still and silent except for her barely audible breathing. He panted heavily and was almost completely out of breath as sweat started to form on his brow. He knew it was a long shot but it was her only chance; it had to work.

He reached into his pocket and pulled out her crucifix by its chain; he'd already cleaned the blood off it in the hospital toilets while he'd been waiting. He lent over the bed and fastened it around her neck where it belonged. He steadied himself against the rail on her bed before bending over and gently kissing her on the forehead.

"I'm so sorry," he whispered. "Please be okay."

He was weak and unsteady but he managed to find his feet and stumble out of the room.

He had to support himself against the wall almost all the way back to the entrance but amazingly he reached the car park without anyone asking what he was doing there or, maybe more importantly, why he was trying to leave the hospital when he was clearly unwell! He turned round and gave one last look at the large building before shaking himself down and pulling out his mobile phone to call up a familiar name from his contact list.

"Hi, Mum, it's me. Listen, it's a long story but could you come down and pick me up from James Cook Hospital, please? No, I'm fine, don't worry…"

As Amy slept silently in her room alone, a smile began to creep across her face.

--The End--